THE EX-WIFE

LYNDELL WILLIAMS

The Ex-Wife by Lyndell Williams

Ramadan Nights Series

©Published by Deen Love Books

All Rights Reserved

The Ex-Wife is a work of fiction. Names, characters, places, and incidents either are the product of the author's imagination or are used fictitiously. Any resemblance to actual persons, living or dead, events, or locales is entirely coincidental.

Any unauthorized reprint of use of this material is prohibited. No part of this book may be reproduced or transmitted in any form or by any means, electronic, or mechanical, including photocopying, recording, or by any information storage without express permission by the publisher.

Edited by Fahmida Bheekoo-Zeidan

Cover by Layla Poulos

ISBN 9798808382527

www.laylawriteslove.com

❦ Created with Vellum

1

ARRIVAL FLIGHT

Zaynab's heart skipped each time the airplane bumped onto the asphalt runway as it landed. She took a deep breath and gazed out the tiny window, her insides bursting with excitement that she was a little closer to her precious Beni. The plane landed and moved to a crawl. She looked down at the cellphone cradled in her palm. Her son's adorable face beamed at her. It felt like forever since she got to touch him.

Beni grew so much over the almost two years that she left him with his father, too long of a separation between mother and child. His face had changed from the precious infant one she kissed the last time she held him. She couldn't wait to do it again.

The plane came to a stop, and passengers jumped out of their seats, pulling down luggage from the overhead compartments before crowding the narrow plane aisle. Zaynab sighed and looked behind her at the surly faces of people struggling with their bags. "Ugh, great," she mumbled, as she smoothed her rumpled clothes and picked up her small, black leather knapsack from under the seat in front of her. "This is going to take forever."

Her phone's familiar chime made the already tight muscle at the base of her neck throb. She hit the green button and put it to her ear. "Salams, Abo. I'm getting off the plane now."

"*Salams. Good, because I'm here.*" The roughness in his tone was most likely the result of him having to tackle city traffic. A born and raised suburbanite, Fahad Nair couldn't stand it. "*How long do you think it will take?*"

"Not long," she lied to him and herself as she waited for the man in the section across from her, yanking to get a too large suitcase out of the compartment. "*Sabr*, Abo. I'll get my suitcases from baggage claim and meet you outside of Gate C." She rubbed the back of her neck and squeezed past the man. "Excuse me," she said, bumping his taller and wider frame. No time to avoid casual touch. He scowled down at her. "Sorry," she mumbled, and continued down the aisle and out of the plane. She made a mad dash through the terminal before pacing back and forth in front of the grinding baggage claim carousel. "Come on. Where are they?"

Her phone chimed a different ringtone. She stopped tapping one of her flats on the terminal floor and answered, a big smile on her face. "Salams, Faiza."

"*Salams.*" Faiza's bubbly voice was a welcome departure from Abo's grumpy tone. "*Did you land?*"

Zaynab continued to scan the carousel. "Yes, just now. I'm getting my luggage."

"*Great. When are you coming over to see Beni?*" The sound of children laughing and banging toys around filtered through the phone.

"I wish it could be now." Zaynab spotted her large white suitcase flying through and landing with a thud. She strode toward it, picking it up and waiting for the rest. "My father is picking me up. I'm going to my parents' house. Can I stop by tomorrow?" She grabbed another piece of her matching luggage set.

"*Absolutely. Why don't you come by around four o'clock? You can stay for dinner.*"

"Alright," she said, grunting as she pulled up a long sleeve and reached for another suitcase. "I'll see you then. Should I bring anything?"

"*Just yourself. I'm sure he can't wait to see you. Beni, guess who's coming over. Mommy Zay.*"

The sound of Beni's cheers made Zaynab's heart flutter. "*Yay, Mommy Zay!*" Beni's squeal came through the phone.

Zaynab smiled. "Aw. I can't wait to see you, Beni. I better hurry up and get these bags to the curb before Abo has a fit. Love you guys." She gave them salams and hung up before dragging a few more suitcases from the carousel and walking to a row of luggage carts. She eyed her bags and then the tiny cart, groaning. No way would she be able to get all of it to the curb by herself. She preferred to travel light, but coming back from overseas meant a list of stuff that her mother wanted—more like demanded.

You can't get this stuff in the States. Om's words echoed in her mind along with childhood memories of her parents paying tons of money for porters to lug around things her mother just had to have from Kuwait.

Zaynab put her hand on her hips and stared at the mountain of luggage. "Now I understand why this drove Abo crazy. Only one of these are mine." She waved at a porter in a black vest and pants. "Excuse me. I need help."

The tall man smiled at her. "Hello, ma'am," he said, dipping his head and touching the brim of his black baseball cap. "I'm happy to help." The hard-shell cases made a loud bang as he piled them onto a massive metal cart. She handed her credit card to a man in a white dress shirt standing at a kiosk. After paying, she followed the porter out of the airport.

She wove through bustling travelers, inhaling car exhaust fumes from the bumper-to-bumper traffic creeping in front of the terminal. She searched the parked and double-parked cars while taking out her phone and hitting the speed dial for Abo.

"Salams," he answered, sounding more irritated.

She returned salams. "I'm outside. I'm wearing a burgundy hijab." She tucked her headscarf along her jaw and looked up and down the terminal. "Can you see me?"

"Yes," Abo said. *"Stay right where you are."*

She offered the porter a sheepish grin. "He'll be here soon."

"No problem, ma'am." The porter flashed a reassuring smile.

Her father's black SUV swerved between two cabs and parked a few feet away from them. The headlights flashed, and Abo got out of the car, stretching and strutting on his long legs. He always walked like a man who owned the world. His scowl disappeared as he got closer. A smile stretched across his light tan face as he lifted his arms and called out, *"Binti."*

Zaynab rushed into his large, welcoming arms. "Salams, Abo." The press of his powerful arms pressed all the air out of her lungs, and she'd have it no other way. She looked up into a pair of piercing black eyes, glistening with love.

"Ah, it's good to have you home," Abo said, as he reached behind his back and pulled out his wallet.

Zaynab held up a hand. "I already paid, Abo."

"Good." Abo opened his wallet and walked to the porter, greeting him. "I need all those in the trunk, please." He pulled out a fifty-dollar bill and folded it before pressing it into the porter's hand.

The porter made a slight bow. "Yes, sir," he said, before pushing the cart toward the car.

Abo pressed a button on his key fob, and the trunk door lifted open. "Get into the car, *binti*." She obeyed, settling into the passenger seat and soaking up the reality of being back after so long in Kuwait. The porter stacked all the bags inside. Abo pulled out another bill and gave it to him. "Thank you." The car swayed as he got into the driver's seat. "Your mother made your favorites for dinner." He squinted at the traffic. "Hopefully, we'll make it home before everything is cold."

Zaynab nodded. "Inshallah." She looked at the porter waving at them. "You tipped him a lot."

"There were a lot of bags," Abo said. He turned the car into traffic. "I had a feeling your mother's list would require a lot of them."

She chuckled. "Yes, it was like I was shopping for the Queen of England."

He shook his head. "I don't get it. We visited you in Kuwait less than six months ago, and she brought back enough to fill Cleopatra's barge." He sighed and stopped at a traffic light. "As long as she's happy." He glanced at Zaynab. "Are you happy to be back?"

She looked down and brushed her black slacks. "I missed Beni, and you and Om."

He turned and peered into traffic. "But you don't miss being here?"

She shrugged. "I do. A little, but I'm still trying to find where I belong."

He grunted. "You've been searching for almost two years. Isn't that long enough?"

"Abo, I—"

He raised a palm. "Let's not get into this now." A large horn blared behind them as the light turned green. Abo pounded on his horn and grunted. "I can't stand city traffic."

Zaynab sunk deeper into her seat and closed her eyes. Abo was always a man who knew who he was and his place in the world. He may love her, but he would never understand that she still struggled to find hers.

2

PAINTED MAN

Xander turned on the engine lights and blew the horn, laughing as the young children—in their kufis and hijabs—surrounding the firetruck covered their ears and cheered. It was the third school demonstration he did that week, but he never grew tired of seeing the wonder in their eyes. He turned everything off and climbed down. "All right, kids. Thanks for coming. Everybody got their bag?" The kids nodded, lifting the little plastic bags filled with paper and toys.

His partner Faiza walked to his side. "Great," she said. "Take them home and read what's inside with your family, so everyone can learn fire safety." The kids closed in around them. She giggled. "I knew we weren't getting out of here that easily. Get ready for the questions."

A little girl tugged at Faiza's sleeve. "Are you really a firefighter? And you wear hijab?"

Faiza put her hand on the small girl's head. "Yes." Her brown face beamed with pride. "I can still do my job in hijab. Muslim women in hijab do all kinds of things." More inquiries followed. Xander watched as Faiza continued to answer the barrage of questions about her with poise and grace. A Black woman hijabi firefighter was a rarity, thrilling the children at the Islamic school.

Xander felt a small, chubby hand pulling on his long thermal shirt. He looked down to see a boy in a white kufi. "I know you," the student announced. The puffy cheeks on his plump white face grew into spheres. "You're the painted man we see at the mosque."

An older boy stood in front of him. "Wait, are you Muslim?" The boy tilted his head and pointed at the black geometric pattern covering the back of Xander's hand just below the wrist. "You're Muslim and you have tattoos?"

A girl with round brown eyes pushed the boy's hand down. "You're so rude, Altaf. Muslims don't have tattoos."

Xander's skin prickled, and he could feel the heat rising up his neck. He filled his chest. "I'm Muslim." The din of chattering kids around him stopped, and all eyes landed on him, including Faiza's, filled with sympathy.

The brown-eyed girl pursed her lips with doubt. "Are you sure?"

Xander laughed. "Yeah, I'm sure."

"He's Muslim," the first boy said, pointing up at Xander. "I've seen him at the masjid praying. He wouldn't pray unless he was Muslim. He's painted all over. I've seen it when he makes wudu. Show them."

The subsequent begging by the surrounding students only fed the nervous energy surging through Xander. He raised his palms and opened his mouth to deny their request, but Faiza stood in between him and the crowd of young gawkers. "Brother Xander came here to teach us about fire safety. Does anyone have questions about that?" The parking lot went silent. "Okay, then let's thank him for coming and let him get the firetruck back to the station to be ready for the next emergency. Give him salams."

The children gave salams in unison and formed groups around their teachers. Some of them kept looking back at him as they lined up and filed into the Islamic school. "Thank you," Xander said to Faiza as soon as the last line of students disappeared behind the large metal doors.

"No problem," she said, unbuttoning her bulky, beige turnout coat with yellow and silver stripes across the arms and chest. "Kids see something different about someone, and they zero in." The school door opened. Faiza's husband walked out, smiling and waving. She waved back, calling out salams. "There's Mansur."

He approached and kissed Faiza on the cheek before holding out a hand to Xander. "Salams, man. How are you doing?"

Xander pulled Mansur into an embrace, returning his salams. Mansur was one of the few brothers who openly accepted him when he moved to town to start his new job at the station. He looked down at the shorter man. "I'm good, alhamdulillah."

"How did the demonstration go?" Mansur wrapped an arm around Faiza's shoulder.

"Fine," Faiza said, smiling at him. "Are you finished teaching the next generation history?" She brushed a brown finger against Mansur's light tan cheek. Faiza was a consummate firefighter with a will like steel, but she was always a little softer and mushier when her husband was around.

Mansur hugged her tighter. "Yes. Your demonstration was the last thing for the school day." The muffled sound of a bell ringing got louder when someone opened the door. "See, they're all coming out." He lifted his messenger bag. "I'm all packed and ready to go home. Did you bring your car?"

"No," Faiza said. "I had Xander pick me up in the truck so I could ride home with you."

Mansur took her hand in his and brought it close to his lips. "I love the way you think, Mrs. Saleh."

Xander tapped Mansur's shoulder. "I hate to interrupt—" he pointed at a small crowd of teachers staring at them "—but I don't think those educators appreciate your public display of affection in front of impressionable students."

Mansur belted out a laugh and nodded toward his colleagues. "True." He brought Faiza's hand down. "We'll finish this at home." He took a step away from Faiza.

She glared up at Xander, playfully. "How are you messing up my game, brother?" she asked, the corners of her mouth twitching.

Xander crossed his arms. "Hey, I was just making an observation." He and Faiza hit it off from the first day he started at the department. She was like a little sister to him.

She pointed at the doors. "Well, instead of observing, you better get in the truck and split before you face another inquisition."

Xander looked toward the doors and spotted the little boy who called him "painted man" running out of the building and straight toward him. "Uh-oh." He opened the truck's door with the words Mastic Fire Department written on it. "Time to go." He pulled himself up with the grab bar and got into the driver's seat. "I'll see you tomorrow."

Mansur looked between Xander and Faiza. "Did I miss something?"

Faiza smoothed a hand over his tie. "I'll explain it to you later." She hooked an arm around him. "Where's your car?" she asked before giving Xander salams and walking across the parking lot.

Xander closed the door and started the engine. Fortunately, a teacher stopped the boy before he could barrel across the parking lot to the truck. Xander honked the horn one last time for the kids and drove out of the circular driveway as buses lined up in an arc along the perimeter.

He turned the corner. His phone rang a familiar tone. He pulled his Bluetooth from his pocket and put it in his ear. "Hey, Ma."

"Hi Xander. I'm so glad I finally got through to you." The formality in his mother's tone indicated that she was none too pleased with him at the moment. *"I was so worried that I was about to send your father to your apartment to check on you."*

"No, you weren't." Dad's voice cut through the phone, filled with irritation.

"Shut up, Frank!" his mother shouted.

"Leave the boy alone, Lydia. He'll come over when he wants."

Xander shook his head. Frank and Lydia Heath bickered like an old TV couple, but they loved each other. "Don't worry, Ma. I'll come over tomorrow night before work."

His mother huffed. *"Well, if it's too much of a hassle to see you parents…"*

"It's not a hassle. I was planning on coming to visit before Ramadan."

"Rama-what?"

Xander glanced up at the roof of the truck before turning a corner. "Ramadan, Ma. It's the month of fasting. It starts in two days."

"Oh, when you starve yourself for thirty days? Has it come around again already?" His mother made it a point not to learn a thing about Islam. As far as she was concerned, her son was born Christian and would die Christian.

"Yeah, Ma. It starts in a few days. I'll spend a lot more time at the masjid—"

"Maasjid?" Ma said with a note of confusion.

"Mosque. Muslim church."

"Oh, okay."

"Anyway, I'll come see you and Dad. It's not a hassle. I want to see you guys, okay?"

"Alright, son. I'll make you something to eat."

His stomach growled in approval. He also went from Xander to son, which meant that her irritation had waned. "That sounds great. I'll see you later. Love you, bye." He hung up and stopped in front of the station, backing the truck inside. Once he spent the required time with his parents, he could enjoy a nice, quiet Ramadan with no drama.

3

WELCOME HOME

"Oh, wow!" Zaynab walked into the foyer and stared up at the silver lanterns banding the ceiling. "Om has done it again." She unwrapped her hijab and pulled out the tight bun at the base of her neck, letting her long, brown hair cascade around her shoulders and down her back.

A sense of childhood familiarity and security infused her at the sight of old Ramadan decorations. She inhaled the delicious smell of food permeating the downstairs of the house. Her stomach growled and heart swelled with content. Kuwait helped her overcome months of depression and anxiety, but it felt so good to be home.

"That she has," Abo said with a groan as he hauled a bunch of suitcases inside and dropped them around his feet.

"Be careful, Fahad." Om rushed into the foyer. Her silver-streaked black hair flowed behind her. "There are fragile things inside." She stopped in front of him.

Abo wrapped his arms around her. "Ah, but none as fragile and precious as you, my dear wife." He laughed as she squirmed and then settled in his embrace. He kissed the tip of her nose.

Om brushed her palms against Abo's chest. "You know, our daughter is right here."

Abo smiled. "She's used to it, right, *binti?*"

Zaynab grunted and reached for her suitcase. "Yes, and I've had my fill. You two continue. I'm going to my room."

"Wait." Om pushed at Abo's chest. He dropped his arms. The fluted sleeves of her tailored kaftan swayed as she raised her arms at Zaynab with a huge smile on her face. "Hug your mother first. You've been away for so long."

Zaynab embraced her mother, loving the warm feelings surging between them. Maybe it would last beyond her homecoming moment.

Om held Zaynab at arm's length. Her arched black eyebrows knitted over her brown eyes. "Hmm. I see your grandmother still feeds you well." She cupped Zaynab's chin and moved her head from side to side. "Your face is rounder."

Zaynab clenched her teeth and forced a smile, trying to ignore the crack shot about her weight. So much for the warm feelings. "I guess."

Om brushed Zaynab's cheek and clicked her tongue. "And you've been out in the sun too much. Are you still using the cream?"

"No."

Om frowned. "No? Why not?"

Zaynab lifted her bag in a huff. "Because I like my skin the way it is." She looked down at her light tan hands, satisfied that she had dumped the skin lightening creams months ago. "I'm going to unpack."

"But—"

"Leave her alone," Abo interrupted, putting an arm over Om's small shoulders. "She's fine. I like it." He gave Zaynab a reassuring smile. "It reminds me of when she was little."

Zaynab turned on her socked feet and rested a hand on the oak banister. She climbed the central staircase, remembering how she and her brother used to slide down it. She stopped at the top and set her suitcase on the landing before turning. "Hey, is Ali coming for Ramadan?"

Abo's face screwed into a frown. "Who knows? He does what he wants."

Om hit Abo's shoulder. "Leave him alone. He's living his life the best he can." She pointed up the stairs at Zaynab. "You need to be worried about her, leaving her family to—" she made air quotes "—find herself."

Zaynab pressed her short nails into her palms, trying her best not to roll her eyes. As usual, she was in the hot seat while big brother Ali got to gallivant and act up. "Look, Om—"

"Now," Abo said, raising a palm. "We won't have any of that." He stroked Om's cheek with a finger, smiling down at her. "Our daughter just got home after being away for a long time. Let's enjoy having her back." He took a suitcase in each hand. "Where do you want these, *habibti?*"

Om pushed a lock of her long salt and pepper hair behind a small shoulder and sighed. "Fine. Put them in the family room." She glided toward the kitchen. "I'll go through them later. Dinner will be ready in an hour."

"Do you want me to help, Om?" Zaynab asked, forcing herself to offer the woman who birthed and raised her the courtesy she deserves, despite the potential for more snark and criticism. Zaynab's gut churned with stress that her mother might say yes.

Om waved a hand and said, "No, I got it. You get freshened up."

Zaynab looked over the banister and watched Om disappear through the arched entry into the kitchen. She let out a sigh of relief and met Abo's gaze. He winked and went into the family room.

Zaynab pulled out the handle to her suitcase. The wheels

clicked on the oak hall floor as she made her way to her room, passing rows of Arabic calligraphy lining the corridor's pristine white walls. So many times, she raced up and down the same hall. First, as a little girl, then a moody teenager, and now, she was the divorced daughter in her thirties, a shame to the family.

She opened the bedroom door, dragging the case inside, leaving it next to the door after she closed it. The smell of fresh linens greeted her. Everything was the same as the day she left to marry Mansur at the spinster's age of thirty. Her socks rubbed against the cream rug as she crossed the room, taking the hijab from her shoulders and draping it over the ecru parson's chair in front of the vanity. She climbed into the middle of the queen-size black wood sleigh bed in the room and flopped backward onto layers of pillows. One fell directly onto her face. She took a deep breath and held it down, screaming until she ran out of air. Hot breath spread across her cheeks. She inhaled again and let out a louder scream, thrashing her legs in the air and then splaying her limbs, letting them go limp. Maybe coming back was a mistake.

If only she hadn't missed Beni and her family so much. In Kuwait, she was the American relative visiting, not the failure who threw away her marriage and child. She didn't have to explain to anyone there that she ran so fast from Mansur and Beni because she suffered with a suffocating drain and struggled with dread from feeling trapped in a loveless marriage. Mansur and she liked each other well enough in the beginning. They bonded over the pressures each of them endured from their parents to accept their arranged marriage. After they wed, the realities of married life weighed on them, resulting in constant arguing. Mansur's misery and the demands of an infant nearly destroyed her. She did the right thing by leaving.

Zaynab tossed the pillow from her face and stared at the ceiling as she brushed wisps of hair from her eyes and forehead. No. She made the right choice coming back, even if it meant brushing off Om's disapproving comments. They would fade away. Om was a splendid mother, but her tendency to pass judgment drove everyone crazy, especially Zaynab—who was often her main target.

Ali's ringtone played in her pants pocket. She reached in and got it, answering. "Salams, flake. You have some nerve not being here."

Ali's laugh floated through the phone. *"Salams, sis. I see you're in your usual mood."*

Zaynab propped on an elbow. "Do you blame me? I wasn't home for two minutes, and Om started with the comments. You were supposed to be here to deflect them."

"Give me a break, Zaynab. You're over thirty. Why do I have to keep running interference between you and Om?"

She glanced at the door, hearing someone coming up the stairs. "Because you keep her off my back and I keep Abo off yours," she whispered. "Which is probably why you're not here."

Another chuckle from Ali floated into her ear. *"Smart woman, but don't worry. I'll be there in a couple of days when Ramadan starts."*

"Good. You're staying the whole month?"

"Let's not get crazy. I have work."

"You're a remote tech specialist. You can work from anywhere."

Ali scoffed. *"Yeah, and do you know how hard it is for me to work there with Om hovering and smothering?"*

"She does it out of love."

"It's still stifling."

Zaynab rolled her eyes. "Fine, but you have to stay at least three weeks."

"*Two.*"

"Done. If you're not here for the first day of fasting, I'm hunting you down. Salams." She hung up and rested her head on a pillow, massaging her temples. Ali always had a nonchalant attitude about Om and Abo's disapproval, unlike her. He was older and male, which meant he could do no wrong in Om's eyes, again unlike her.

Zaynab sat up and climbed off the bed. She peeled her blouse from her tired arms and walked toward the bathroom. She undressed and reached into the white-tiled shower, turning on the water and holding a palm up to the cold water raining from the shower head. Once the water warmed, she stepped under it, glancing at the built-in shelves with the same black and white-patterned tiles as the ones on the floor. A brand-new shower puff sat next to body wash on the middle shelf. Above them was a folded washcloth, another example of Om's careful mothering. She wet the washcloth and squeezed body wash on it, making a foam before gliding the suds over her body. "I'm here to enjoy Ramadan with Beni," she told herself as she scrubbed hours of travel off her. "I don't care if Om never gets over me divorcing Mansur."

She rinsed and dried off, crossing the bedroom and opening the closet to a row of clothes. Scent from the cedar slats bombarded her nose. She pushed the clothes along the rod and examined each of the inside outfits hanging in front of the pants, skirts, blouses, and abayas she wore outside. One thing she got from Om was a love of clothes. She moved the outfits one by one, stopping at a floral, Dashiki style kaftan. She plucked it from the closet. The perfect thing to relax around the house in after being crammed in a human sardine can. It was important to relax before seeing Beni tomorrow.

She tossed the kaftan on the bed and went to the vanity

for a wet brush. After she brushed her tresses and put them in a bun, she put on underwear and donned the soft fabric, allowing the kaftan to cascade over her body. "I'm a new person. A better person, stronger."

She slipped on the house shoes near the bedroom door and turned the knob, "Everyone will have to get used to it."

4

THE HEATHS

Xander parked by the curb and glanced at the brick-faced rambling ranch in the middle of the tree-lined suburban street. He grabbed the potted orchid from the leather seat and climbed out, rounding his black Ram 1500. The headlights and white lights spanning the roof blinked as he pushed the lock button on the fob.

The evening wind blew through the trees and past him. He stepped onto the soft grass before standing on the sidewalk, staring at his childhood home. Dad prided himself on the perfectly manicured lawn. He talked with the other men on the block for hours about the best way to care for it. Xander continued up the cement walkway and climbed the porch steps, flanked by Ma's beds filled with flowers and shrubs, their colorful petals visible in the fading daylight.

Xander knocked on the door and rolled up his sleeves. He took a deep breath, inhaling the delicious aromas permeating from the house. Promise of Ma's cooking and seeing his family made the trek to the next county worth it, and truth be told, he missed his parents. The door opened and flooded him with more smells and light. Ma stood in the doorway, dressed in shoulder-less top and jeans tight enough to show off her ability to keep her shape despite having three kids scattered across the country and one grandchild.

"There you are!" Ma raised her arms. "I almost thought you weren't coming." She put her arms around him.

Xander bent and gave her a hug. "I'm not that late, Ma."

"Twenty-minutes. That's more than late enough. Do you arrive late to a fire?"

He kissed her cheek and chuckled. "Well, since no one schedules those, I can't possibly be late." He held up the orchid. Its soft white and lavender petals swayed in the indoor lights. "For you." He presented the plant, his inside fluttering like he was ten again, seeking to make her happy.

Ma clapped her hands together. Her lipstick-stained lips formed an 'o' and brown eyes lit up. "Oh, Xander! It's beautiful." She took it from him and held it up in front of her face. "I love it, and I appreciate you remembered not to get me a bouquet." She turned in her furry slippers and walked further into the house.

Xander followed, stopping to take off his shoes and leaving them with the others. Only a fool would trek through Lydia Heath's abode in street shoes. "I remember. Bouquets die. You want something you can keep alive." He grabbed his house shoes from the shelf next to the door and slipped them on before following her into the living room.

Ma set the plant on the bay window between a prayer plant and potted lilies. She put an arm around Xander's waist as he approached. The top of her head barely reached his shoulder. "Such a thoughtful gift." She cupped a flower in her small hand and smelled. "I love orchids. Come—" she patted him on the back "—you deserve a meal."

"I do," he said, following her out of the living room and down the short hall leading to the kitchen. "What you got?"

"Your favorite," she said over her shoulder. "I made lasagna and garlic bread."

"Where's Dad?"

She scoffed. "Where do you think? Planted in front of the TV, watching documentaries."

"I don't see what's wrong with that. He's retired now..." Xander frowned and peered at his ex-girlfriend, perched on a stool at the black quartz peninsula that reached from the wall to the middle of the kitchen. "Violet?" he asked, stopping on top of the white tiles.

Violet offered a coy smile, tossing her long black hair over her back and letting it cascade down to her behind. "Hey, Xander." She waved and leaned on the counter, propping her delicate chin into her palm. "Nice to see you." Her brown eyes flashed before she dragged her gaze up his body. "You're looking good." Her lips curled into a seductive smile.

Xander clenched his fist and relaxed the frown on his face. "Yeah, thanks." He turned to Ma. "Can I talk to you for a minute in the den?"

Ma stopped and knitted her eyebrows. "Now? Dinner is almost ready."

He put a hand on her shoulder and turned her. "It's important. Excuse us for a minute, Violet," he said, before guiding his mother past the peninsula and through the entrance to the den. Inside, Dad sat in the middle recliner of the light brown sectional sofa in front of a huge plasma TV. Sounds of a World War One battle blasted from it. Dad turned to them and grinned. "Hey, son." He yawned and stretched his long legs and arms. "How's it going?"

"Good, Dad," Xander said, before stopping behind the wall so they would be out of Violet's line of sight and earshot. He spun and bent so he and Ma were eye to eye. "What's she doing here?" he asked with a loud whisper, jabbing a finger toward the kitchen.

"I invited her," Ma said. "I figured since you were coming over, it would be nice for the two of you to see each other."

"She doesn't belong here, Ma. She's my ex. We don't need to see or have anything to do with each other."

"You guys are always breaking up. You've been on and off again for five years."

"Well, we're off permanently now."

Ma crossed her arms. "Oh, really? Violet told me you didn't take back the engagement ring you gave her."

"I let her keep it. I figured it was the right thing to do. It doesn't mean that I still want to be with her. We want different things."

"I disagree. You two were in love and wanted to start a life together before you switched religions." She lifted her chin. "Besides, Violet and I grew close over the years. You can't just expect me to turn off my feelings for her, even if you have."

Xander raised his arms in the air and dropped them. "I don't believe this. You can't still be close to my ex, Ma. There aren't any kids."

"I think she's a nice girl, and I don't intend on throwing her out onto the streets. So, you will have to just be nice during dinner." Ma twirled and strode into the kitchen. "Can you help me get dinner on the table, Violet?"

Xander leaned and watched Violet hop off the table and round the peninsula. She glanced back at him and winked. He sighed and flopped on the sofa next to his father and popped out the recliner's footrest. "Unbelievable."

"I don't know why you think it's unbelievable," Dad said, reaching over and opening a small cooler on the end table. He pulled out a can of beer and handed it to Xander.

Xander shook his head. "No, thank you."

"That's right, you don't drink anymore. I bet you can use one now, though." Dad's belly shook as he guffawed and popped open the beer before taking a swig. "Look, your mother is having a hard time with your conversion."

"And you're not?"

"Not like her. You know I'm not very religious, but she is. She keeps hoping you'd come to your senses and return to Christianity."

"That will not happen."

Dad burped into his fist and looked at the screen. "Maybe not, but until she comes to accept that it won't, you're going to have to deal with stunts like this." He pointed behind himself just as Violet came in and stood over them.

"Frank, Xander, dinner's ready." She smiled, wiping her hands on a dish towel, looking very domestic.

Dad smiled up at her. "Thanks, angel. We'll be right there." She walked out of the room. Dad glanced at Xander and laughed some more before drinking his beer.

Xander shook his head. "I'm glad that this amuses you."

"Hey, she's not my ex."

"Let's go, Frank!" Ma bellowed.

"We're coming, Lydia!" Dad yelled. "Just hold your horses." He put down the recliner and stood, beer still in hand. "Come on, son." He clamped down on Xander's shoulder. "If you eat fast, it'll be over sooner."

Xander stood. "Yeah. I'm going to have to talk to Violet."

"Fine, but save that for after dessert. I want to enjoy my meal, even if you don't." Dad clamped down on Xander's neck.

"Okay, Dad," Xander said, allowing his father to steer him toward the kitchen table. His stomach churned with apprehension. Tonight's dinner would not be with no indigestion.

5

A CHANCE

Xander leaned on the front doorjamb and crossed his ankles, straining to keep dinner in his gut as he watched Violet hug Ma under the porch light. Lasagna and chocolate mousse churned as she kissed his mother's cheek and wrapped an arm around her shoulders.

"Thanks for having me, Lydia. Everything was delicious." Violet lifted a paper shopping bag filled with containers. "And thanks for these—" she giggled "—I won't have to cook for days."

Ma laughed and passed a hand down Violet's long hair. "You're welcome, sweetie. Remember to bring the containers back." She turned to Xander. "Why don't you be a gentleman and take the bag to the car for Violet?"

"Could you, Xander?" Violet asked, panting and placing the bag next to her feet. "It is kinda heavy, and I'm exhausted from work."

He pinned Violet's gaze. The glowing smile on her face used to go straight to his heart, endearing her to him. Now, it only produced more guile, upsetting his stomach further. He straightened and said, "sure" between his clenched teeth. He reached past Ma and snatched up the bag. The containers rattled inside. "Let's go." He rushed down the stairs and strode down the walkway, stopping at the sidewalk. "Where are you parked?"

She stood in front of him and pointed a manicured finger down the street. "Around the corner."

He scoffed. "It figures."

"What do you mean?"

"Nothing." He strode in the direction she pointed, using his long legs to his advantage. The crisp evening air didn't help cool his distemper or the misery tightening his chest that things were about to get messy. As if the breakup wasn't hard enough, with her crying and shouting. Violet was determined not to let go, but he was equally determined to shake her off.

"Hey!" Violet called out to him, her heels clicking on the sidewalk. "Wait up!"

He ignored her, turning the corner and searching the rows of cars for a red one with decorative eyelashes on the headlights.

"Please, Xander—" she tugged on his arm "—why are you being so rude?"

He stopped and turned, peering down at her. "Why are you here? We aren't in a relationship anymore. You shouldn't be hanging around my parents."

"I like your parents."

"Oh, please. You and I both know that you're staying in contact with my mother to get to me."

She stepped closer and looked up at him. "Is that so bad? I still have feelings for you. I won't apologize for it."

"You don't have to apologize, but nothing is going to happen between us. It's over."

She sneered. "Why? Because you say so? We were happy, and then you became Moozlem—"

"Muslim."

Her beautiful features contorted. "Ugh, whatever. All I know is that I was planning a wedding, and you come home saying you can't eat pork, putting your head on the floor and claiming that you can't be with me anymore. Do you know how much that hurt?"

He sighed and relaxed his shoulders. "I'm sorry I hurt you, but I wasn't happy. Part of me felt empty for years. I was just going through the motions, doing what I thought everyone expected of me. Then I found Islam."

She raised her hand. "Please, I've heard it all before."

He started walking toward her car. "Then you know that living with you was wrong. We weren't married. It took me a while to get the strength to leave. I loved you back then."

Her heels clicked faster as she rushed to keep up with him. "Then why don't we get married? We planned to anyway."

He stopped at the car and put the bag on the hood. "That was more than a year ago. I've moved on. You should too. I want a Muslim wife and family."

She stood so close to him they almost touched. The streetlight shone on her flawless skin. "Maybe I can be your Moozlem wife. I can learn about Izlam—" she cupped his cheek and stroked it with her thumb "—then we can be together like we're supposed to."

Xander closed his eyes. Her warm, soft touch felt wonderful, familiar. For years, Violet's arms gave him solace from the world. Here she was, ready to open them and embrace him. How could he resist? He took her hand and gently put it to her side. "I know you aren't interested in Islam. Remember, I tried to tell you about it."

Violet batted her lashes and swayed in her spot. "Well, maybe I changed my mind."

He leaned on one leg and stuck a thumb in the loop of his

jeans. "Look, if you're truly interested in Islam, visit the local mosque and get some information, but understand that becoming Muslim doesn't mean that we will get back together."

She hooked a finger in his belt. "So, there's a chance?"

He pulled her hand out. "Probably not. Right now, I'm concentrating on my faith. I'm not looking to get married to anyone." What a punk answer, but part of him couldn't stomp on her heart. He picked up the bag. "Unlock the car, so I can put this inside." He put the food in the back seat.

Violet rounded the car, the streetlight shining on her frowning face. She opened the driver's door and looked over the car at him. "I'm still interested in learning about Islam."

"Okay. There is a mosque not too far from here."

"Do you go to it?"

"Not since I moved, but they can help you."

Her bottom lip poked out. She shrugged. "Alright. Can you text me the address?"

"I don't have your number anymore."

She beamed. "But I have yours." She pulled out her cell. "I'll call you, so you have mine again."

He scratched his head and primed his mouth to tell her he didn't want her number. It took him months to delete it. "Violet." He sighed. "Never mind. I'll text you the information." Although doubtful, she may have a genuine interest in Islam. Who was he to block her path? Besides, he could always delete it after. His phone rang in his pocket. He didn't answer.

Violet pressed a finger on her phone's screen. "There, now you can send me the information or anything else you want."

"Just the information, Violet."

She nodded with her lips pulled into a half smile. "Yeah,

okay. Goodnight." She got into the car and started the engine.

Xander watched her drive down the street before pulling out his phone and staring at the tiny familiar numbers glowing on the notification screen. He came so far over the past couple of years of being Muslim—new job, new home, new life. He put the phone in his pocket and jogged back toward his parents' house. Violet needed to face facts. He was no longer the same man that she loved.

6

BENI

Zaynab tapped the steering wheel of her father's SUV while she sat in front of the red light. "Oh, come on," she mumbled to herself. It seemed like every light she came to was red, making it take longer for her to get to Faiza and Mansur's house to see her precious Beni.

The guilt for leaving him with his father ate away at her for a long time. A person shouldn't have had to choose between her child and sanity. It wasn't until after sessions with Dr. Shah that she realized that on top of her marital problems; she was suffering from postpartum anxiety, which made everything so much worse.

The light turned green and her already thumping heart beat a little faster. "Yes, thank you. Almost there." She steered the car through traffic, getting more excited each time she passed a familiar landmark that showed she was closer. After a few more turns, she drove into the cul-de-sac. She parked in front of Faiza and Mansur's house and stared at it. Her nerves fired, making her gut churn. She opened the door and got out. Her designer heels clacked on the cement as she rushed round the front of the SUV and up the driveway. "Oh,

Darn it." She stopped in the middle and clenched her eyes and fist before turning and lightly jogging back down. She swung the passenger door open and grabbed the shopping bag full of gifts. "Keep your head straight, Zaynab."

She reached the front door and knocked. The anxiety surging through her made her light-headed. Everything felt unreal. Or had everything been a dream? She wiped a hand on her sweaty forehead, just below the hem of her hijab. The door opened. Faiza stood behind the screen door with a huge smile on her lovely face. A puff of thick black coils sat on top of her head like a crown. She held her baby Bushra on a hip.

"Hey," Faiza said, pushing the screen door's black handle. "As-salam alaykum. You're early."

Zaynab stepped inside. "I know. Sorry. I just couldn't wait to see Beni."

"Aww. I understand, but Mansur took Beni with him to get flowers."

"That's okay. It'll give us a chance to talk." Zaynab smiled at Bushra and took a hold of one of her tiny feet dangling at her mother's side. "Salams, little one. I'm your Auntie Zaynab." Bushra stared, then smiled at Zaynab. "Oh, she looks just like her grandmother. Adiba must be so happy."

Faiza giggled and hugged Zaynab's neck, kissing her cheek with a pair of soft, full lips. "Trust me, she is. I have a hard time keeping my baby with me when she's around." Faiza's printed maxi dress swayed around her legs as she walked further into the house.

Zaynab kicked off her shoes and followed, walking into the living room. She stopped in front of the overstuffed beige sofa and sat the bag on the glass coffee table next to an open coloring book and crayons. "I brought gifts for everyone."

Faiza bent in front of the bag. "That's so nice. You didn't have to."

"Yes, I did." Zaynab pulled out a wrapped box and handed

it to Faiza. "Sweets from Kuwait. I thought it would be nice to have them after dinner." She took a deep breath. "It smells wonderful."

Faiza held the box in front of her. "Alhamdulillah. We're having meatloaf."

"Yum." Zaynab took a cloth doll with no face and a hijab out of the bag next. "This is for Bushra. It's handmade. I thought of her as soon as I saw it in the market." She held the Muslim doll in floral patterned clothes in front of the baby. "Do you like it, Bushra?" The baby laughed and grabbed her gift, inspecting it.

"I think she likes it. Thank you." Faiza sat on the sofa and put Bushra next to her. "So, tell me. How does it feel to be home?"

Zaynab took a seat beside them. "Nice. I missed it, especially Beni. Honestly, he's the only reason I came back."

"Really?"

"I think so. My parents came to Kuwait a few months ago. They visit every year, so I could see them. I got to heal and figure a lot of things out. I'm not Zaynab the failure over there."

Faiza put a hand on her lap. "You're not a failure here, either. You needed to save yourself so that you could be a better mother to Beni."

Zaynab fiddled with the hem of the doll's clothes. "Yeah." Some may think it was weird for her to open up to her ex-husband's wife, but Faiza was a good friend to her when she was at her worst. She also took care of Beni after the split.

The screen door flew open. "Mommy!" Beni shouted as he ran inside. "I got a flower!" He disappeared behind the side chair and reappeared on the other side, stopping. The smile on his chubby, light tan face faded. He stared at them, his small mouth agape. He backed up slowly.

Mansur stood behind Beni, stopping him. "Hey, look who's here. It's Mommy Zay."

Faiza got up. "Don't be scared, sweetie." She took one of Beni's hands. "You remember Mommy Zay—" she tried to lead him to the couch "—you see her all the time on the phone."

Beni snatched his hand away from Faiza and wrapped his arms around Mansur's leg, burying his face in the fabric of his father's black slacks and crushing the daisy in his little hand.

"Oh, boy." Mansur dropped two bouquets on the side chair and stroked the top of Beni's head. "It's alright, son." He picked up Beni, who crushed his burgundy dress shirt in a palm. "Mommy Zay is back to see you."

Zaynab raised her arms and smiled as Mansur moved closer to her with Beni. "Salams, baby. Come, give me a hug." Her heart sank when Mansur bent over her, trying to pass her the toddler, and Beni clung to him tighter, whimpering. She had video called him every chance she could while she was away, so he wouldn't forget her. It must not have worked.

Mansur's thick brows knitted. He tried to loosen Beni's grip on his neck. "C'mon, Beni. Don't you want to give Mommy Zay a hug?"

Zaynab touched Mansur's arm and shook her head. "No, don't force him," she said with a shaky voice, trying to blink back the tears welling in her eyes.

Faiza approached and stroked Beni's back. She opened his tiny fist with her delicate brown fingers and took the crushed flower out of his hand. "It's fine, sweetie. Mansur, why don't you take him to wash up for dinner?"

Mansur nodded and hefted Beni over his shoulder. "C'mon, little man. Let's get ready to eat." He pulled Beni's shoes off his tiny feet, and the two of them disappeared upstairs.

Zaynab sobbed and sniffed, sitting back down. "Dr. Shah warned me that this might happen." Anxiety welled into a knot in her chest. Bushra crawled toward her and pulled up on her shoulder, smiling. At least she wasn't a total pariah.

Faiza sat next to her. "What did your therapist say?"

"That the only time Beni has seen me over the past two years was on a screen, and that it might take some time for him to get used to me in person. Who am I kidding? I abandoned him. No wonder he wanted nothing to do with me."

Faiza touched her knee. "You did what you had to. I remember how bad things got for you."

Zaynab put a hand over Faiza's. "It was. The depression had me questioning my sanity, and it got harder and harder to take care of Beni. But I'm better now, and I want to connect with my son."

"Did Dr. Shah give you any suggestions?"

"She said to keep spending time with him, and that he'll come around."

Faiza stood, picking up Bushra and putting her on her hip. "Then that's what you'll do. Why don't you come over and have iftar with us during Ramadan? That should help Beni get used to you."

Zaynab rose and faced her, tickling Bushra's tiny chin. "I couldn't impose on you guys," she said in a cooing tone. Bushra shrugged and giggled.

Faiza raised her free palm. "Don't worry about it. We all want what's best for Beni and having a relationship with you is an important part of his life."

The sound of Mansur coming down the stairs drifted to them. He reappeared with Beni still over his shoulder. He stopped next to Faiza, putting his son down and resting an arm on her shoulders. "An important part of whose life?" he asked, his thick black eyebrows furrowed as he looked back and forth between Faiza and Zaynab.

"Beni's," Faiza said, reaching down and stroking her stepson's soft, curly hair. "Zaynab's therapist suggested she spend as much time as possible with Beni. So, I invited her to join us for iftar during Ramadan."

It tore Zaynab inside to see her son run and hide behind Faiza, the mother he knew. She wiped the tears from her cheeks. "I can't intrude on you guys every night."

Faiza gazed at Mansur. "It will help them reconnect."

Mansur's lips flattened into a thin line while he rubbed Faiza's forearm. "That's true." He took Bushra and held her up in the air, looking up at her giggling face as he spoke with a light pitch. "So, it's settled." In response, Beni peeked from behind Faiza's dress, staring at Zaynab like she had three heads.

Faiza turned and walked to the kitchen entryway. "Okay. I'll put dinner on the table." Beni ran behind her.

Mansur picked up a bouquet from the side chair. "Beni, wait—" he crouched down "—give these to Mommy."

Beni looked at his father and Zaynab, standing as if it scared him to move. Finally, he ran to Mansur. "Okay, Daddy." He snatched the flowers and raced across the room and shot through the kitchen entryway.

Mansur handed Zaynab the bouquet of lilies in his hand. "These are for you, from Faiza. She remembered that they're your favorite." She took them and thanked him. He turned his head toward the kitchen before sighing and flopping in the side chair. "I thought this would be easier." Bushra lay the back of her head on his chest.

Zaynab sat on the sofa and put the flowers on the coffee table. "I had hoped it would be. Even though I ran away from him, I never stopped loving him."

Mansur scratched the top of head. "You ran away from

me more than him. When you needed a husband, I wasn't a good one. I was so caught up in feeling sorry for myself that I neglected you and your disorder. I'm sorry for that."

"I know. You've told me before. It took me a long time to stop being angry with you."

Mansur grinned and pointed at her. "Yes, but you eventually let that anger go, and your son will get over his fear of you too, inshallah. It'll just take some time. Don't worry. You'll come here and wait for Beni to gravitate toward you."

She offered Mansur a smile, despite her churning insides and the nagging thought that Beni would never want to come near her. No, that was the anxiety talking. She had to be more positive. "Yes, thank you for letting me."

"Dinner's ready," Faiza called from the kitchen.

Mansur hit the arm of the side chair with his hand and got up. "Let's go. Your journey back into Beni's good graces starts now."

"Okay." Zaynab took a deep breath, freeing up as much of the tightness in her chest as possible, and followed Mansur. This had to work.

7

RAMADAN, NIGHT ONE

Xander lifted his head and turned it to the right and left, finishing the evening prayer. The scent of the masjid's incense filled his nose along with the smell of musky attar oil the brothers had a habit of sharing during congregational prayers. He shook the hand of the man to the right of him and then the one sitting on his left side, touching his hand to his heart after each time. People padded in their socks and bare feet across the ornate carpeting. He watched as they crowded, not at the exit door, but the one leading to the upstairs dining hall.

His stomach growled. The pre-dawn meal for the first day of Ramadan kept him going for most of the day, but his now empty gut demanded food. Like at his old masjid, this new one offered break-fast iftar meals every night, making it easy for him to eat a meal after a long day of going without. It wasn't the longest fast he ever completed. When he first became Muslim a few years ago, Ramadan arrived during the summer. The cooler, shorter days of spring were a welcome relief to getting up to eat at three o'clock in the morning and not having a bite or sip until after eight. He rose and ambled toward the crowd of men. One stood in the same corner he did every time Xander, and he was both at prayer.

The older man rubbed his salt and pepper beard, staring daggers at Xander with a pair of piercing black eyes. What was his deal, anyway? Xander's nerves prickled his skin. As he got closer to the crowd, he tugged at his thermal shirt sleeves. They covered much of his tattoos, but not all. The ones on the back of his hands still showed along with those around the bottom of his neck, making him an oddity, surrounded by people with unmarked skin.

"Brothers!" a man bellowed at the entryway. "Form a line! No one eats unless they're in line!"

Xander chuckled and shook his head at the familiar scene. It was probably the same at masjids across America and the world. Hungry Muslims pushing their way to their first meal. He got in line and shuffled closer to the open french doors, silent while everyone spoke with each other in different languages. The aroma of spicy food intensified the nearer he got to the tables, making his stomach rumble more. He grew up a typical white boy, so the rich spices and heat took some getting used to, but now it didn't feel like Ramadan unless his tongue was burning at least a few times. He missed some good ole American dishes by the middle of the month, but he could forgo them, so he wouldn't have to eat alone. He pulled his phone from his cargo pants, not noticing the usual stares whenever he came for prayer.

His ink didn't faze all the brothers. They were more interested in saying their prayers and heading out the door to get on with their lives. Still, a few found him strange enough to stare or glare at him to express their shock and disapproval that he dared entered Allah's house with tattoos. Normally, gawking didn't bother him. He had grown used to encountering the occasional public ogler, but at the masjid, it filled him with discomfort. It brandished him in some people's eyes as less Muslim and not to be trusted.

A text message notification dropped from the top of the screen. He grunted at Violet's number.

Violet: *I had fun the other night.*

He shuffled with the line of men and tapped on his phone screen while climbing the stairs.

Xander: *Sorry. I forgot to send you the information for the local masjid. I'll do it now.*

Violet: *Oh, okay.*

He rolled up his sleeves and searched in his contacts, copying the information for his old masjid and pasting it to a message for Violet. Small talk would only encourage her that they still had a chance. Best to keep communication direct and short.

Xander: *There you go.*

Violet: *Thanks! Can I call you if I have questions?*

Xander: *The imam or some sisters there should be able to answer your questions. Good night.*

The message notification dinged again. He pressed the *block* button and shoved the phone in his pocket.

"Here, brother," a voice said. A short man held a cream paper takeout box to him. Xander made the last step up and took the box, thanking the man, who mumbled "you're welcome" while staring at Xander's neck.

Xander expanded his chest and walked into the dining area filled with white resin picnic tables loaded with men. The open mini blinds covering large windows bordering the hall revealed the darkening night. He scanned the tables for a clear spot. The men had grouped together according to common nationality. At a few tables, South Asian men in baggy cotton shalwar pants and long kameez tops that reached their knees sat with others wearing dress shirts and slacks. A din of Urdu bloomed from them.

It was the same for another cluster of tables with men speaking in Arabic. Next to it was a table filled with Black men. Xander breathed a sigh of relief. It was his experience that African and African American men proved to be more open to strangers. He plastered on a smile and wove through the tables, each one falling silent as he passed, only to get noisy again in a foreign language. He couldn't understand what they were saying, but he knew it was about him.

The Black men all watched at him as he approached. A brother with a round, brown face and broad nose smiled. He stood and raised a hand. "As-salam alaykum, brother," he said in a thick northeastern American accent. "Ramadan Mubarak."

The greeting to have a blessed Ramadan set Xander's heart at ease. He clasped the arm firmly and shook it. "Wa alaykum salaam, and Ramadan Mubarak." The man pulled him into a warm embrace. "I'm Xander," he coughed out between firm pats on his back. The rest of the men dropped their food and got up to offer him more hugs before he finally had time to sit. He opened the lid to his takeout tray, smiling at the thick cubes of butter chicken swimming in a spicy red sauce. One of his favorites. "Alhamdulillah."

"Yes," said a brother with a narrow face and Nubian nose. He spoke with a strong Nigerian accent. "The food is always good at the beginning of Ramadan." The table burst into a bout of laughter.

Xander joined the men, laughing, before he pierced a piece of chicken with his fork. The men, all from different backgrounds, talked with him, none of them staring at or asking him about his tattoos. He enjoyed the reprieve.

~

Xander finished the last prayer for the night and pushed up on his knuckles, straightening into a standing position. He stretched his achy limbs. This time, he wouldn't wait for the crowd to thin. Instead, he wedged past men yawning, talking and massaging their arms and legs, everyone looking weary after hours of standing for the special Ramadan late-night *Tahajjud* prayer. He squinted in the dim lighting and focused on the large glass exit doors, opening and closing automatically as people poured out into the darkness lit by strings of lights hanging between the parking lot's light poles and draped on bushes lining the edge of the property.

Xander scraped his heels on the plush carpeting and plodded onto the cold entryway tiles, stopping at the wall of steel shelves crammed with shoes. He bent and scanned over dress shoes, designer sneakers, and worn pairs of sandals on the bottom shelf. He spotted his black tactical boots and reached for them, stopping when someone stood in front of them. "Excuse me," he said, holding his hand in midair. The legs in a pair of dress slacks hadn't budged. He cleared his throat and repeated his words, saying, "excuse me" louder. The person remained motionless. Xander saw a pair of feet in black socks and dragged his gaze upward as he stood and came face-to-face with the brother who stood in the corner earlier that evening.

The man's eyes narrowed and bored into Xander. "Tattoos are haram," he said, his face twisted with contempt.

Xander balanced on one leg and rolled up his sleeves before crossing his arms over his chest. Here we go again. The only thing worse than people staring at him was when one of them confronted him filled with self-righteousness. "So is not minding your own business."

"Every time you come here—" the man pointed at

Xander's neck "—you distract everyone with those. We come here to pray, not look at how you defiled your body." He puffed his chest as other men stopped their progress out of the masjid and gathered in front of them. "Why would you do that to yourself?"

Xander dropped his hands and balled his fists. The older man wasn't the first to chastise him about his tats, and he wouldn't be the last. If this was at his old masjid, when he was a new Muslim, he would explain the reason for his tattoos, but those days were over. He owed no one an explanation. He stepped closer and stared down at the slightly shorter man with a groomed salt-and-pepper beard. "You going to move or what?" Grumbles came from the surrounding men. He refused to even glance at them. They didn't matter.

The older brother closed the remaining distance between them until his chest bumped into Xander's. "No, not until you explain yourself. Are you even Muslim?"

Xander clenched his teeth. The peace that had come from hours of praying evaporated, replaced by anger that anyone would dare question his Muslimness. He should back away, diffuse the situation and avoid hurting anyone, but the fury burning in his gut made it difficult.

"Brothers!" Imam Jobe shouted from the other side of the entryway. The crowd divided, revealing the imam in a white thobe and black leather socks. He strode through the opening, concern covering his dark brown face. He reached them and put a hand on each of their chests. "Please, stop this. It's Ramadan."

"I'm trying to leave!" Xander took a few steps back and broke the stare down between him and the man. He looked at Imam Jobe, a thin man just as tall as him, and took a deep breath. The imam was one of the few people who openly accepted him when he moved to town. He calmed a little and continued. "I was leaving when this—" he frowned at the older man "—brother came up to me running his mouth."

The other man lifted a palm toward the crowd. "I'm just saying what everyone else is thinking. You shouldn't be here."

Imam Jobe shook his head. "That's not true. Brother Xander is just as welcome in Allah's house as anyone else. He's our Muslim brother." He patted the man and Xander on their shoulder. "Why don't we go talk in my office?" The man moved with Imam Jobe toward the hall leading to the imam's office.

"I can't," Xander said, snatching up his boots. "I have to get to the station for my shift."

Imam Jobe nodded and smiled. "Of course. We won't keep you. Perhaps we can schedule for some other time?"

Xander propped on a wall. "Yeah, that will not happen," he grumbled, tugging on his boots while the sounds of people speaking Arabic and Urdu floated over him. He tied the strings and stomped the rubber soles on the marble floor before squaring his shoulders and glowering at the crowd of men still watching them. Each time he made eye contact, the person would look away and move to the side. There would be no masjid spectacle for them to soak up tonight. Xander stormed through the opening in the crowd and strode out the automatic doors. Unbelievable. Even after being Muslim for years, he still had to struggle. He made his way across the parking lot, filling his tight chest with the night air.

"Brother!" Imam Jobe called out, "wait!"

Xander stopped at his truck and clicked the fob. He turned to see the imam rushing toward him as the crowd spilled out of the entrance doors and spread out into the parking lot. The latest drama over, the men went to their cars. Xander leaned on his and waited.

Imam Jobe stopped in front of him, panting. He was still

amazingly spry for his age. "Listen, I think you should really set some time aside to talk to the brother."

"Why?" Xander seethed. "So I can explain myself to him?" He looked over Imam Jobe's shoulder. The man stood at the edge of the parking lot, staring in their direction. "No disrespect, Imam. I'm not doing that." He opened his truck door. "As-salam alaykum, Imam." He got in and started the engine, watching the imam walk back toward the masjid.

Xander backed out of the parking stall. The truck's headlights shone on the man. What a piece of work. Xander drove out of the parking lot, determined to not let one close-minded man or anyone else blow his peace any longer.

8

TIPPING OVER

"Look, I said I was sorry." Zaynab turned the box wrapped in blue paper with pictures of stars, crescents, and camels on the kitchen table and broke off a piece of transparent tape from the dispenser. She looked up at Ali. He stood on the other side with his legs spread apart and fists on his hips. "I need to spend as much time with Beni as possible."

Ali pouted. "We had a deal."

"I know, I know, but that was before I realized how hard it would be to reconnect with him."

"What deal?" Om asked, as she entered the kitchen and stopped in front of the stove. She lifted the lid on a huge stainless steel stock pot. A plume of steam burst into the air. The delicious aroma of all the food cooking filled the room and made Zaynab's stomach rumble in protest that she would miss another of her mother's sumptuous meals. It was worth it, though.

Zaynab leaned to one side of Ali to get a better view of Om. "Nothing," she said, before taping down the last triangular flap.

Om looked at them over her shoulder and then rolled her eyes at the ceiling. "Fine—" she tapped the spoon on the pot's rim and replaced the lid "—you two keep your little secret." She turned and approached them. "Before you go Zaynab, I want to talk to you about this nice man who is looking for a wife." She took her cell phone out of her kaftan pocket. She swiped the phone's screen, her eyes squinting with determination. "Now, where is his picture?" Om got closer. Zaynab backed away, hitting the chair behind her. Om paid no attention. Her face brightened. "Ah, here it is."

Zaynab's temples throbbed as Om held the phone in front of her face. A man stared at her with smoldering eyes. A thick, black mustache graced the top of his full lips and a five o'clock shadow covered his square jaw. He was gorgeous, and the same as the others. All Zaynab saw was another potential jailer, trapping her into a chaotic relationship. She tore her eyes away and met Om's gaze. "No, Om," she said with a firm authority that sent the message that neither the man on the screen nor her marital status was up for further discussion.

Om frowned and tucked the phone back in the pocket, defeated. She returned to the stove.

Zaynab went back to the table and Beni's gift. "Look, Ali, I'm keeping up my end for our deal. Aren't I here all day?" She turned the box again and inspected her wrapping job. Hopefully, the magnetic building block set would interest Beni enough to put together a castle with her, ending night after night of him hiding behind Mansur or Faiza

Ali took a few steps back and leaned on the island, separating the dining and cooking areas. "Yeah, you're here when Abo is out or resting. When he's home for iftar, that's when he lays in on me."

Zaynab chuckled. "You sound like you're ten. I have to do this. Beni is still timid around me. I need to spend time over there so he can get used to me in his life."

Om scoffed, folding her arms. "I don't see why you can't just bring Beni over here." She propped her hands on the kitchen island and pressed her lips with determination. "We're his family too."

Zaynab squeezed the bridge of her nose and buried the desire to remind Om that neither she nor Abo tried to see Beni while she was overseas. Instead, they mailed him Eid gifts and kept their distance. To do so would start a fight that she had no time for. She lifted the box. "Yes, but Dr. Shah said that Beni and I should interact in *his* environment until he's comfortable." She hefted the box higher in her arms. "I'll bring him here once he is, inshallah," she called over her shoulder as she entered the foyer. Maybe that was a good enough answer for Om, and she wouldn't follow her.

"And how long will that take?" Om asked, approaching Zaynab from behind.

Zaynab put the box on the floor next to the door and turned. "As long as it takes. We can't rush this. It will only cause more problems."

Om squinted. "So, you plan to go over there every night during Ramadan? You're going to wear out your welcome."

Zaynab sighed and picked up the hijab she left on the banister earlier. "Faiza and Mansur said I'm always welcome." She draped the hijab over her head, working to prevent Om's disapproving stare from making her simmering anxiety any worse.

Om waved a hand. "Oh, please. They're only being polite."

"No, they want what's best for Beni, just like me. I'm his mother. I belong in his life."

Om raised her chin and spun. "For now." She walked back toward the kitchen.

Zaynab trailed behind her. "What's that supposed to mean?"

Om spoke as she made her way back to the stove. "It

means—" she bent and opened the oven "—you'll be in his life until you decide you can't handle it and fly back to Kuwait." She took a huge, black-covered roasting pan from the oven.

Zaynab stopped in her tracks and held her breath. The homey warmth surrounding her turned cold. She glared at Om. "That's not fair. You know why I left."

Ali strode across the kitchen and stopped at Zaynab's side. "C'mon, Om. That's a low blow."

Zaynab crossed her arms and smirked. "Those are the only blows she gives."

Om dropped the pan on the island and put her hands on her hips, her face screwed with irritation. "Is this where you try to blame me for everything?"

"No, but—" she stopped talking when she heard the front door opening.

"Salams!" Abo called out before appearing in the kitchen doorway. He glanced around at everyone. "Everything okay?" Tense silence surrounded them.

Om sighed and took the cover off the pan, revealing a roasted leg of lamb. Abo walked toward her. She tilted her head, accepting a kiss from him. "Yes, fine."

Abo grinned and hooked an arm around Om's waist. "Good. It's been a long day, and I want to come home to peace."

Om pulled open a drawer, removing a pitchfork. "Zaynab was just leaving to see her son."

Abo's brows rose. "Again?"

"Yes." Zaynab backed away from them, turning her head at the muffled sound of her phone ringing in her purse on the entryway table. "And I'm running late." She got her phone from her handbag. The name Sabrina shone on the screen. She hung her handbag over her shoulder and answered. "Salams. Hold on a sec." Mercifully, the call ended the conversation and subsequent guilt trip from her parents. She retrieved Beni's gift and gave salams, bolting out the front door and to her car. "Okay," she said, tucking her phone under her hijab and next to her ear. "How are you?"

"*Alhamdulillah, good,*" Sabrina answered. Her British accent came through the phone. "*Are you busy?*"

Zaynab hopped into the car. "I'm on my way to see Beni."

"*How's that going?*"

"Slowly." Zaynab turned out of the block.

"*He's still scared of you?*"

"Yes, but I'm going to be patient until he comes around. How are things going with you?"

"*I can't complain. Marriage and The Family is doing well. I wish you could come on the podcast for an episode.*"

"I'm sorry. I know I said that I would do it, but things became hectic."

"*It's fine. You needed to concentrate on your son.*"

"Thanks for understanding." Zaynab filled her lungs and loosened her grip on the steering wheel. Sabrina was a good friend since they connected through one of her popular Muslim podcasts. She was a straight shooter and tremendous supporter. Even though they never met person-to-person, they were close. "I wish Om would."

"*She's bugging you about getting married?*"

"Practically since I landed. She just ambushed me with a pic. I got the heck out of there."

"*I bet you did. Are you sure you're not interested?*"

She pursed her lips and wove through traffic. Sabrina never brought up marriage before. What was her deal now? "Maybe one day, but not with one of Om's and Abo's arrangements. I want there to be a spark, you know."

"*Yeah, I know. Arranged marriages and dating set-ups may work for some people, but not everyone. I remember you mentioning that on the show.*"

"Exactly. Their arranged marriage ended well. Om and Abo are deeply in love and happy, but for me, it's once bitten, twice shy. Anyway, let me know how I can make it up to you."

"Are you saying that you owe me one?"

"Yup."

Sabrina made an over-maniacal laugh. *"I'm going to have to give this some thought."*

Zaynab giggled. "Something tells me I'm in trouble." A small, gray sports car swerved in front of her from the lane to her left. She screeched and slammed on the brake, steering away from the car. The SUV's tires hit the curb. Her heart raced as it tilted with her inside. "Allah!" She slammed her eyes shut. Was this how she was going out? Because of some idiot? The driver's side of the car hit the blacktop. Metal crunching against asphalt blended with her screams. After the car stilled, she opened her eyes, watching the gray car's brake lights darken before it peeled away and disappeared down the road.

9

EXTRACTION

*X*ander yawned and stretched, moving the swivel chair under him back and forth. He rubbed his weary eyes and pushed the keyboard out of the way. He opened the marble composition notebook and rested his arms on the long Formica table that stretched along the wall of the fire station office. "Okay, let's get this done." He picked up his mechanical pencil and copied the next line of Arabic words in the textbook propped up on the black computer monitor. Pencil lead scratched on the paper. Although his mind imagined him creating letters as pristine as those in the book, the reality of what his hand created differed vastly from it. He finished the first word, a bumpy defilement of the language.

The late nights of prayer and work made it difficult to continue his studies, but he was determined not to flake again like he had when he moved to town. Fortunately, things had been slow at the station during Ramadan. He could get some studying done after finishing his shift tasks. He glanced down at the empty chairs running the length of the table. Even though the office was empty, he preferred the workstation furthest from the door so he could concentrate. He wrote another line of Arabic, this time a little better than the last. "Alhamdulillah," he said, straightening his back. He touched the pencil to the next clean line but stopped when his cell phone rang. "As-salam alaykum," he said after answering.

Mansur returned salams. *"How are things going? Hey, no running in the halls."*

"Good."

"I called to invite you to our house tonight for iftar. Faiza tells me you go to the masjid to eat every night."

"Yeah, I'm heading there when I finish my shift."

"Come to our house instead."

Xander spun in the chair and walked to the wall of windows. He peeked through the opening of the white mini blinds. Late afternoon light streamed on him as he gazed at the pedestrians passing the station. It would be nice to sit and eat without people staring. He tolerated them every night because it was better than eating alone in his apartment. "Okay. Jazakallah. I just need to finish up some stuff here."

"Alright. I had to stay at the school late, but I'm on my way home now. See you there."

"Salams." Xander hung up, sat back at the desk, and put a finger on the textbook, ready to copy the next line.

The office door flew open. "Hey, Xander." Justin leaned against the open door. "There is a car accident on Monroe. Can you help?"

Xander shot out of his seat. "Sure. How many vehicles?" he asked as he passed Justin and rushed down the hallway.

"Only one. An overturned SUV."

∽

Zaynab inhaled and coughed out the acrid air. She lay inside the car, tilted on its side as a crowd of legs filled the windshield, and people talking and yelling filtered to her. Despite her heart pounding, encouraging her to try to get out, the ache in her chest and apprehension coursing through her kept her immobile.

A woman bent in front of the windshield. "Hey, can you talk?" she asked, pushing her long black hair from in front of her face.

Zaynab raised her head from the side curtain airbag that deployed during the crash and pushed down the steering wheel, the front airbag pressed against her chest. "Yes. I think I can unbuckle myself." She reached to her side for the seat latch.

"No," the woman said, raising her hands. "Wait. A fire truck is coming."

The sound of a siren blared in the distance and grew louder. A large fire truck with its lights flashing stopped a little way down the street. A team of firefighters jumped off and jogged to her. Zaynab lay her head back down and took a deep breath. Tears spilled from her eyes, blurring the view of the crowd moving away, and firefighters approaching the car in big boots. One of them bent and met her gaze. Tattoos peaked out from the collar of his tee shirt and decorated his bulky arms. "As-salam alaykum. Can you speak?"

"Wa alaykum salam. Yes." Zaynab blinked away the tears and focused on his face. He was Muslim?

"Don't worry. We'll get you out." The confidence in his beautiful brown eyes calmed her. "Stay still." His face disappeared as he stood and shouted orders and walked away. "Let's set the vehicle back on its wheels, then we'll extract her." The firefighters lined up along the SUV.

Zaynab's nerves fired at the car rocking, and the sound of

crunching metal and cracking glass. She reached around the airbag and clenched the steering wheel. The firefighters grunted, pushing the car until it swayed and groaned, finally teetering on its tires and dropping straight.

The driver's door flew open. The firefighter from before pushed the side curtain airbag away. He smiled at her and then dipped his head, bending further into the car and examining her body from head to toe. "I think it's okay to get you out now."

She threw her shaking arms around his neck the moment he backed away. The fear trapped inside released, causing her to sob. "Don't leave me."

A brawny arm wedged between her and the seat while another wrapped around her front. The firefighter unlatched the seatbelt. "It's okay. I got you." He scooped her out of the car. Zaynab held him tighter, burying her nose against his neck. The smell of cologne and sweat filled her nostrils. He walked with her in his arms. She let go only after he set her down on the back of an EMT truck.

"Thank you," she stammered, putting her hands on her lap. She gulped for air and to calm herself.

"You're welcome." A smile spread over his firm jaw. "Now, let me check you again. Do you feel any pain?"

"Just a little in my chest." She looked over his shoulder at the crumpled side of the SUV and groaned. "I'm doing better than my father's car."

He glanced over his shoulder. "Yeah. The pain is probably from the airbag hitting your chest. You should let us take you to the emergency room."

She heard her cell phone twittering in the car and shook her head. "No. I have to go see my son." She tried to get off the edge of the truck, but he stopped her, a stern but compassionate expression on his face.

"You may have internal injuries. It's best for you to go."

She searched his handsome face, softening to the authority in his tone. "Okay, I'll go, but can I get my phone and stuff out of the car?"

"You can," a police officer said as he ambled to them, "after you talk to me."

"I will, officer, but I need to call the people who are expecting me." And she had to call Sabrina, who must be worried sick.

The cop took out a pad and pen, not even looking at her. "Let's finish this first."

The phone stopped. Zaynab slumped her shoulders and searched the darkening sky. "I was driving down the street, and a car shot out in front of me." As she explained what happened to the police officer, the tattooed firefighter walked toward the car, disappearing behind the cop. The police officer asked her a bunch of questions. When was he going to be done already?

The crowd spread until there were only emergency workers in the street talking and guiding traffic. After a while, the firefighter reappeared, carrying her purse, cell phone, and Beni's present. He stood next to the cop, who closed his notebook. "We're done. You can make your calls now." He handed Zaynab a piece of paper with a bunch of numbers on it and told her what she needed to do to get the police report. She thanked him and watched him walk away.

"Here." The firefighter sat the box in the truck and put the purse on it before holding up her phone in front of her. "They're going to take you to the ER."

She accepted the phone. "Alright." A pang of disappointment struck her that he wasn't taking her. "Jazakallah." She thanked him in Arabic to confirm that he was Muslim. She shouldn't care, but for some reason, she did.

"Alhamdulillah," he said, backing away from her. "Good luck." The call to prayer echoed in a pocket of his beige turnout pants. He grunted and took it out, turning on the heel of a boot and striding away.

Another emergency worker approached her. She followed their directions and got into the EMT truck. She settled on the gurney inside and searched the contacts on her phone for Sabrina. Zaynab filled her friend in, then dialed Faiza's number. She held the phone against her ear, watching an EMT moving around the ambulance. The car accident was bad enough. How long was she going to be stuck in the emergency room? So much for seeing Beni tonight.

10

EMERGENCY ROOM

Xander stretched his arms and legs and settled back in the hard seat. He stared at the double doors leading to the inside of the hospital's emergency room. They opened. He sat straight. Maybe they finished with her already. A nurse in scrubs, pushing a patient in a wheelchair, strode out of the doors and toward the glass exit. Xander huffed and leaned back into the chair, crossing his arms over his chest. How had he ended up waiting for a woman he didn't even know, anyway? Faiza, that's how.

He couldn't say no to Faiza. Once he returned to the station, he called Faiza to let her know he was going to be late because he had helped with an accident. It turned out that she knew the woman he pulled out of the SUV and had just gotten off the phone with her.

Zaynab is Beni's mother. Faiza's frantic voice echoed in his mind. *Can you go to the ER to make sure she's okay? I'll have Mansur contact her family.*

The doors flew open again. Xander closed his eyes, refusing to see who was coming out. His stomach growled. He rubbed it. He could have at least been smart enough to eat before he left the station or stop off somewhere and grab a bite to break his fast, but no, he had to rush straight to the hospital. Another, longer grumble prompted him to stand up and head straight for the vending machines in a small room at the end of the rows of seats. There probably wasn't much to choose from, but it was something. He tugged his wallet from the back pocket of his jeans and examined the snacks offered on the other side of the glass. Nothing but an assortment of junk food, not fit enough for a meal. He pulled out a debit card and slid it through the small black slot. Desperate times called for desperate measures. *I'll hit a halal spot after I make sure whatever-her-name was okay.*

"As-salam alaykum?" a woman's voice said behind him. He turned. The woman from the accident stood, holding a clear belongings bag with the gift he took from the car for her. She smiled up at him, looking a lot less anxious. Her round black eyes sparkled, offering a peace like that of a moonlight sky. "Your name is Xander, right?"

He returned salams. "Yes, how do you know?"

She giggled and showed him her phone. "Faiza told me. She said you were out here waiting for me."

He shoved the card in his wallet. "How are you?"

She put the bag on the floor. "They did a bunch of tests. It took forever, but they said that I'm fine."

He leaned on one of the vending machines. "Alhamdulillah. That's good to hear."

"My chest will hurt for a few days. You were right. It's from the airbag." She pointed at the vending machine glass. "You didn't eat anything?"

"No, but I'm fine. What about you?"

"They gave me some water."

"So, you feasted?"

She laughed and smoothed the floral hijab fabric framing her full cheek. "Yeah."

"I can get you something."

"No, that's alright."

He hit the cancel button on the vending machine and glanced at her again, unable to stop himself from looking at her. Disheveled clothes and harsh hospital lighting didn't take away from her beauty. He shifted his gaze to the floor. "I'll go get something now. Do you have a ride home?"

"My brother is coming to get me." She picked up the bag and walked backward. "I'm going to wait for him outside."

"I'll wait with you."

"You don't have to do that. You've done so much already. I know you must be hungry."

He strode past her. "It's fine. Let's go."

They stood on the curb, watching cars and ambulances pull into and out of the traffic circle in front of the vast building. Xander paced behind her, watching to see if the next car to pull up would be the one to take her away. An uncertainty whether he wanted her to go plucked at his gut. He was not in the market for a wife, was he?

A black Mercedes stopped in front of Zaynab. She smiled back at Xander. "Here's my brother."

A tall man got out and raced around the car. "Salams, are you okay?" He threw his arms around Zaynab.

She hugged him back. "I'm fine. The car isn't, though."

The man frowned. "Don't worry about the car. Abo is doing enough of that for everyone."

"That, I believe." She walked with her brother toward Xander. "Ali, this is Xander. He pulled me out of the car and stayed here to make sure I was okay."

Ali's brows rose. "Wow, talk about going above and beyond." He held out a hand. "Thank you for looking out for my sister."

Xander shook and offered salams. "Alhamdulillah, I'm glad to help."

Ali squinted at him. "You're Muslim?"

Xander pushed down the irritation welling inside from the question. Everywhere he went, there was always someone asking about it. Then came a bunch of asinine questions like: *Do you know Muhammad*, or *Do you know the Shahada?*

"Yes," Zaynab said. "He's friends with Faiza and Mansur."

"Oh, really?" Ali straightened as if he was a drill sergeant at inspection. "Did you convert?"

Xander pulled out his keys. "Yeah." One dumb question was all this guy was going to get. "For a while." He smiled at Zaynab. "I'm glad you're okay. It could've been worse. Assalam alaykum and Ramadan Mubarak."

She smiled back. "Ramadan Mubarak."

He walked away from them. The call for Isha came from his phone. He pushed the button to stop it. There was still time to get to the masjid for night prayer. Then he would clear his friend's hot ex-wife from his head. He would not allow any more distractions to his worship and studies.

11

11-IFTAR

Zaynab fidgeted her fingers over the beat-up box as the car service driver turned the corner. She smoothed a crinkled piece of wrapping paper. After picking her up from the hospital, Ali brought her home, so she missed seeing Beni. By the time she was able to have a video call with him, Faiza told her he was already asleep. Hopefully, missing one day with him would not negate her attempts to get her little boy to come near her.

The car made another turn into Faiza and Mansur's street. She pointed at their house. "Right there."

The driver parked behind a big pickup truck. The driver's door of the truck opened. Xander climbed out.

Zaynab gasped. Excitement swelled in her chest as she watched him strut up the walkway, wearing a pair of jeans and a long sleeve shirt stretching over his muscular torso. What was he doing there? The firefighter who carried her out of the car wreck dominated her thoughts. Om and Abo fawned over her when she got home. Once she assured them that she was okay, she went to bed and lay awake, remembering how Xander looked and felt when he carried her away from the car wreck. Now there he was, looking just as fine as when he rescued her.

"Do you need anything else?" the car driver asked.

Zaynab flinched and tore her gaze away from Xander. "Huh? Oh, no. Thank you." She opened the door and got out, chastising herself inwardly, as she did the night before. There was no time for crushing on anyone. She had to get things right with her son.

She stepped onto the curb of the cul-de-sac and waited while Xander knocked on the door. What could she say to him? They were strangers.

As if sensing her there, he turned on the porch. The effects of his handsome grin reached across the manicured yard and hit her in a way that no other man had in a long time. Her plans to sideline any chance of a love life faded as Xander walked back toward her. He offered salams. "Hey, sis. It's good to see you."

She couldn't help but smile and giggle. "Good to see you, too." What was wrong with her? This is only the second time she's seeing this man but being near him lit an attraction in her that she hadn't felt for anyone, not even Mansur. She didn't know what to do with herself.

Luckily, Mansur came out of the house, holding Bushra. "Salams!" he called out, waving at them. "Come in."

Xander stepped to the side, still smiling. He was just being nice. She was reading too much into a friendly grin.

Zaynab walked into the house. The scent of comfort food wafting through the house helped ease her angst. She searched the living room. No Beni. She put the box on the floor by the door and smiled, raising her arms to Faiza, who glided toward her.

Faiza gave her a warm hug and salams. "I was so worried about you." Her smile eased Zaynab's nerves further. She held Zaynab at arm's length. "I'm glad you didn't sustain any injuries." Beni came down the stairs and stared at Zaynab before dashing behind Faiza.

Zaynab forced a smile, despite the frustration building inside. He was still avoiding her. Dr. Shah said not to make it a big deal. "Yes." She glanced over her shoulder, watching the men come into the house. "The ER doctors said I was lucky."

"They're right." Faiza put an arm around her and guided her toward the living room. "A car tipping over can be very dangerous, right, Xander?"

Xander nodded. "Yeah. I've seen some pretty bad ones."

Beni shot from behind Faiza and stood in front of Xander with a big smile and his arms in the air. "'Ander. Make me a tree."

Xander chuckled. "Alright, little man." He picked up Beni and put him on his shoulders. Beni giggled with delight and reached for the ceiling, his chubby fingertips barely touching it. "Look, Mommy, I'm a tree."

"Yes, you are, baby," Faiza said. "How is your father handling everything, Zaynab?"

Zaynab sighed. "He said he's just glad I'm okay." She looked at Xander and Beni as she talked. "I offered to pay any deductibles, but he refused." She giggled. "He said to use the money to buy myself a car. I guess he won't allow me to use his ever again."

Mansur belted out a laugh. "I don't blame him." He looked at his watch and patted Xander on the shoulder before handing Bushra to Faiza. "Maghrib is in. I'll call the adhan, then we can eat." He went to the corner of the living room. Xander followed Mansur and sat on the floor with Beni next to him. Mansur raised his cupped hands near his ears and let out a melodious tone.

Faiza tapped Zaynab's shoulder and signaled her toward the kitchen. Once inside, they filled small bowls with food.

"Beni seems to like Xander," Zaynab stacked plump dates on a small silver plate.

"Yes." Faiza arranged grapes and other fruit on a platter. "He races right to him whenever they're at the station, and sometimes Xander comes here to hang out with Mansur."

"He seems very nice."

Faiza picked up the platter and smirked. "He is very nice, and very single."

Zaynab met her gaze. "I didn't ask."

"I know you didn't. I figured I'd volunteer the information." She walked toward the dining room. "Do with it what you want."

Zaynab followed. She couldn't deny that she wanted to do something with the information, but what? Xander was an attractive man, who she just met ten seconds ago. Did she have the guts to express an interest in him? No. That was madness. She would pray, eat and try to get Beni to warm up to her, ignoring the smoking firefighter.

⁓

Zaynab put a forkful of chocolate cake in her mouth and gazed over the dining room table. Xander sat in the living with Mansur and Beni. She watched him laugh and eat, something he'd done all evening.

"You're staring again," Faiza said, sitting next to Zaynab at the table. She smiled and fed Bushra a piece of cake with her fingertips.

At that moment, Xander turned and looked at Zaynab. He glanced away and said something inaudible to Mansur. The distance between the dining room and living room made it hard to hear him.

Zaynab blinked and met Faiza's gaze. "I'm not staring."

Faiza pinched off another piece of cake while Bushra

banged her hands on her highchair. "Okay, whatever you say."

Zaynab leaned closer. "I'm not in the position to think about anybody," she whispered. "I need to focus on Beni."

"So that's what you're going to do? Use Beni as an excuse?"

"He's not an excuse."

"Good, because you can work on your mother-son relationship and still think about the possibilities of a romantic one."

"With Xander?"

Faiza shrugged. "Maybe, or someone else. You're a beautiful Muslimah. It's time to open yourself up. Besides, you're clearly interested in Xander. So, why not explore it?"

"Just like that?"

"Hey, we're Muslim. That's how we roll."

"What if he's not interested?"

Faiza looked in the living room's direction and then back. "Time will tell."

"Time? What time?" Zaynab glanced in his direction, meeting his gaze again. This time, they lingered a little longer. There was definitely an attraction there. But so quickly?

"Baba!" Beni yelled and picked up the present she had left by the door. He toddled back into the living room laughing with glee. "Look! This is mine?" He dropped the box on the coffee table. He and the men leaned over it.

"Yes," Mansur said. "It's from Mommy Zay." He waved for Zaynab to come to them.

She got out of her chair and strolled to the back of the sofa. Beni's eyes widened. She offered him a reassuring smile. Beni shrank against Mansur.

"Why don't you open it?" Mansur asked.

Faiza stood next to Zaynab, holding Bushra with one arm

and stroking Zaynab's back with the other. "It'll be fine."

Beni ripped away the paper. His face lit up. "Blocks!" Mansur and Xander helped him open the box. He turned it upside down. A package of colorful blocks wrapped in plastic hit the table with a thud. Zaynab watched the three of them release the blocks and start building. She wanted so much to join them, but she kept her distance.

Mansur stood. "Um, I'll be right back." He walked around the sofa and tapped Faiza on the shoulder. "Can you help me, *habibti?*" They shared a look.

Faiza nodded. "Sure." They disappeared into the kitchen.

The blocks preoccupied Beni. He hadn't noticed that his father and stepmother had left the room. Normally, he would chase after them when Zaynab was around, but he kept playing.

Zaynab knew they left to give her a chance to get closer to Beni. She took a few cautious steps. If he bolted away from her, it would break her heart, but she had to take a chance. "Can I play too?" she asked in a soft voice.

Beni and Xander stopped. Beni stared at her. The fear of his probable rejection swelled inside her. "That would be great, right Beni?" Xander said in an overexcited tone.

Beni looked between them and then smiled. "Yeah." He lifted a block toward Zaynab. "Here, Mommy Zay. This one is red."

Zaynab's heart leapt. She dashed around the sofa and took the block, sitting on the floor next to Beni. Alhamdulillah, it finally happened. Each block Beni handed her filled her with joy. Every so often, she saw Mansur peeking at them from the kitchen.

They played until the call to prayer went off on Xander's phone. He rose and stretched. "Wow. It's time for Isha already."

Zaynab kept building blocks with Beni, watching his

every move. She stroked his hair and was relieved when he hadn't cowered away from her.

Mansur and Faiza came back into the room. "I know," Mansur said. "It feels like forever for Maghrib to come in, and Isha comes in a flash." Everyone laughed. "Are you going to the masjid?" he asked Xander.

Xander nodded. "Yes, you?"

"I can't. Faiza is working tonight. I'm on dad duty with the kids."

Xander walked to the door and turned, offering Mansur his hand. "Jazakallah, for having me." He looked at Faiza. "Everything was delicious."

Faiza patted Bushra on the back, rocking back and forth. "I'm glad you liked it. Why don't you come again tomorrow? I know you usually go to the masjid, but this is much more comfortable."

"I will, thank you." Xander opened the door. He offered salams and left.

After the door closed, Mansur brushed Faiza's chin with a finger and threw her an accusatory look. "What are you up to, *habibti*?"

Faiza pulled up one corner of her mouth. "I don't know what you mean. Don't you like Xander?"

"Yes. He's a good guy, but—" he looked between Faiza and Zaynab "—okay. I see." He lumbered toward the living room corner. "Let's pray, so you can sleep before your shift."

Faiza yawned and stretched. "Good idea."

Mansur lifted his arms. "Come here, Beni."

Beni ran to his father. Zaynab collected the blocks, putting them in the box. Alhamdulillah, it worked. She was going to connect with her beloved son. Things were looking up. Xander's smiling face as he played with her and Beni came to the forefront of her mind. Maybe in more ways than one.

12

ROASTED

Xander put the cup to his lips. He sipped, letting the drink wash down more delicious food as he watched Zaynab wipe smeared date pulp from Beni's chubby face. She sat poised at the other end of the table; her face bright—beautiful. He never tired of seeing her every night, though it had thrown off his Ramadan.

One night eating at Faiza and Mansur's house was all he expected. He would be in and out. Zaynab showed up at the same time as he, a pleasant surprise, as was Faiza's inviting him to dine with them. He jumped on the chance to eat with his friends and see Zaynab again, crushing his plans to avoid distractions. She was a big one, with her captivating black eyes and enticing lips that drew him into accepting more dinner invitations.

Over the past few weeks of Ramadan, he enjoyed warm iftars with his close friends and her. At first, he and Mansur ate separately from the women, but they moved gradually to the dining table. It gave him a chance to get to learn more about Zaynab. The more he got to know, the more he liked. She was smart, funny and dedicated to her son. Xander put the cup down, not taking his eyes away from her. He tried his best to guard his gaze, but it was hard for him not to concentrate on her graceful movements when she was near. He hadn't been so attracted to a woman since becoming Muslim. Like the grumbling in his gut and dryness scratching his throat during the daylight hours, her presence made him aware of another hunger he had to feed.

Faiza waltzed into the room with her arms wrapped around a big bowl. "All right. Who's ready to stuff their face?" She laughed and set the bowl on the table. Steam drifted up from the mound of yellow rice pilaf.

"I am," Mansur said, following her with a platter laden with a big roast surrounded by potatoes, caramelized onions, and carrots. He set the platter next to the rice. "I can't wait to cut into this. Thanks for bringing it, man."

"Anytime," Xander said. "It's the least I can do since you've opened your home to me for Ramadan."

Zaynab met his gaze. "You made a roast?"

Xander flashed a self-assured smile. "Yes, at work. The station has a fully equipped kitchen."

Her endearing giggle tapped his heart. "So, I guess what they say about firefighters and cooking is true. Impressive."

He rested a forearm on the table. "It's one of my many talents." He flirted openly, something he hadn't done with a Muslim woman until Zaynab. He knew he was establishing an interest in courting her by doing so. Now to see if she was keen to marry, too.

She blinked and looked down with an enticing smirk. "That's good to know."

"Yeah, okay," Mansur said, one eyebrow raised. He picked up a carving knife and fork. "Why don't you come and cut for us?" He pointed the knife handle toward Xander.

Xander stood and leaned over the table, cutting the roast and revealing the light pink inside.

"Alhamdulillah," Zaynab said. "It's not overcooked." She got up with the plate Faiza had placed in front of her, rubbing her abdomen. "I'm famished. I missed Suhoor."

"With the fasting day so long?" Faiza asked. "That must've been torturous."

Zaynab nodded and walked closer to Xander. "It sure was. So, if you don't mind, brother—" she smiled up at him "—I'd like two pieces."

He pierced a slice with the fork. "You got it, sis." He put it on her plate, followed by another. A woman who was not ashamed to enjoy a good meal. That was impressive. He finished serving everyone and sat next to Mansur.

"So, ladies," Mansur said, cutting into his roast. "How's the car shopping going?"

"Excellent," Zaynab said. "We picked out one today. I'm going to get it tomorrow. I don't know what I would've done without Faiza's help."

Mansur looked at Faiza with pride. "My baby knows cars."

"Indeed, I do," Faiza said, lifting her chin and handing Zaynab a small, colorful kid-sized plate. "You made a good choice."

Zaynab took the plate and sighed, furrowing her eyebrows. "Yeah, now to find a job."

Xander swallowed his food. "You're looking for a job?"

"Yes, but not with much luck." She scratched her forehead and held a forkful of meat to her mouth. He noticed her slender fingers quaking. It wasn't the first time. She was one of many for whom life offered sometimes endless tension. He had seen fellow firefighters and family members struggle with similar angst. She took a bite and lay the fork on the plate, flexing her fingers until the shaking stopped. Then she tickled Beni's tummy, having masked the outward manifestation of her inner turmoil.

"So, you're settling here?" Mansur asked.

Zaynab nodded. "I don't want to become a stranger to Beni again. I belong here with him."

"I agree," Mansur said.

"We both do," Faiza added, resting a hand on Zaynab's shoulder. "And I'm sure you'll find something." How nice that Mansur's present and ex-wife had a close relationship. They were both amazing women.

"I certainly need to," Zaynab said. "I want a place for myself, with a room for Beni to come and visit. Living with my parents is …" she looked at Xander and then poked at the rice on her plate. "Anyway, something will turn up."

Mansur wiped his mouth with a napkin. "Listen, they're looking for front office help at the school. Why don't you apply?"

Zaynab stopped poking her food. "The front office?"

Mansur raised a hand. "I know. It's not as lucrative as advertising."

"No, I left the game years ago. I'm not looking to go back. It's way too stressful, and I'm not interested in commuting to the city."

"Okay, then I'll talk to the principal tomorrow."

"That would be wonderful, Mansur. Thank you." She cut into the roast, an exuberance of hope and promise covering her face.

Xander spent the rest of the meal trying to balance his desire to take all Zaynab's attention and keep a proper Islamic personal distance until he officially courted her. One by one, the table cleared of the diners, leaving him on one end and her and Beni on the other. The toddler yawned and stretched; his thick lashes fluttered as his lids drooped closed. "Uh-oh," Faiza said. "I knew this would happen." She stood behind Beni's highchair and popped open the belt. "He missed his nap this afternoon." He kicked his little legs as she lifted him out of the chair. "Let's go, sweetie."

Zaynab stood. "Can I help get him ready for bed?"

"Um, Mansur is upstairs with Bushra." Faiza put Beni on her hip. "He won't be down for a while. Why don't you keep Xander company?" Before Zaynab could respond, Faiza strode away.

"See you later, Mommy Zay," Beni said, waving as he and Faiza disappeared around the corner.

"Okay, sweetie," Zaynab flopped back in her chair. She faced Xander. "So, I guess I'm keeping you company?"

He smirked and pulled his sleeves above his forearms. Faiza was always looking out for him. She obviously sensed his interest in Zaynab. "I don't want to be a burden."

She tilted her head back and laughed. "You know full well that you're not a burden." She put a hand on her belly and poked the untouched slice of roast on her plate with a fork.

"Couldn't finish?" Xander leaned in his chair.

She covered a burp with her hand. "No. I guess my stomach shrunk from all the fasting."

"Probably."

She stared at his arms. Her smile faded, and his nerves jolted. He felt too comfortable around her and exposed the thing he was most self-conscious about. Silence surrounded them. He hiked the shirt sleeves above his elbows and waited for her next response. Better he found out if his tattoos disturbed her before he made his move. She squinted and pointed at his arm, stretching her arm over the table. "Can I ask you a question?"

He swallowed and sat straighter. "What is it?"

"Is that why you always wear long-sleeves?"

He scratched the back of his head. "So, you've noticed?"

She shrugged. "I remember you wore short-sleeves on the

day of the car crash, but you've worn long-sleeve shirts every day, even though it's been warm."

"I guess I have. They've caused a lot of negative attention for me when I'm around Muslims. I can't cover these—" he pointed to his neck and hands "—but I try to conceal as many of them as possible. It makes life easier."

She sucked her teeth and shook her head. "That has to be so irritating. Muslims can be so judgmental, feeling holier than thou just by looking at a person."

"I think that's a human flaw."

"True, but still. We're supposed to be merciful with each other. Your tattoos aren't anybody's business."

"No, but that doesn't stop the stares and comments. I want to concentrate on getting closer to Allah." He slowly blinked. "And other people, at least anyone who wants to get to know me."

She shifted in her chair, looking down and delighting him with an alluring sigh. "Well, I've enjoyed getting to know you. Do you have tattoos all over?" After asking, her light-tan skin brightened from a blush radiating on her face.

"No, just here." He passed his hands over his arms and chest. "I started getting inked when I was a teenager, but I haven't gotten any since I became Muslim."

"I see." She rearranged the folds of her hijab, her gaze remaining fixed downward.

"Do they bother you?"

Her head shot up. Concern covered her face. "Not at all."

He put a hand to his chest and let out an exaggerated sigh. "Good. Now I can rest easy tonight."

She gave him the side-eye. The corners of her mouth twitched. She slapped the table. "Hilarious."

Mansur entered the dining room. "What's hilarious?"

"Nothing," Zaynab said.

Mansur hitched a thumb over his shoulder. "Faiza is getting ready to put Beni to bed."

Zaynab pushed away from the table. "Oh, okay. Can I go up and say good night?"

"Of course."

She got out of her seat and brushed the black, high-waisted designer slacks covering her legs. Xander marveled at the excitement swelling inside him as she closed the distance between them and stood over him, leaning on an arm. "See you tomorrow night?" she asked, with a slight purr in her voice.

Xander nodded. "Inshallah."

She sashayed around him. He forced himself not to stare at her as she gave salams and left the dining room. Amazing how the subtlest movement from her sent him reeling. That she obviously knew her effect on him only made things more exciting.

Mansur's fingers snapped in front of Xander's face. "So —" he sat on the edge of the table and looked down at Xander "—it's clear that you haven't been coming here to enjoy my company."

Xander leaned back in the chair. "Nah, man. It's not like that." He glanced at the corner Zaynab disappeared behind. "Well, not at first. I hope there isn't a problem."

"No problem. Faiza and I noticed that you and Zaynab were feeling for each other over a week ago. I'm just waiting for you to ask me."

Xander shot up his eyebrows. "Ask you what?"

Mansur put a hand on Xander's shoulder. "To introduce you to her father so you can place intentions and see if you want to get married."

Xander filled his lungs and made a heavy sigh. "Everything happens so fast."

"No one is saying that you have to marry her immediately, but you know the rules, no casual dating."

"Yeah, I get it."

Mansur rose and picked up empty plates from the table. "Just let me know when you want to take the next step."

Xander got up and started helping. "Sure thing, man." The speed at which people expected to ask about a woman he met less than a month ago may seem crazy, but it felt right.

13

NEW CAR

Zaynab turned her new car into the fire station lot and put it in park. "I can't believe I'm doing this." She bit her bottom lip, sniffing the new car scent.

"Doing what?" Sabrina asked. Her voice drifted from the speaker. *"You're just showing a friend your new car."* She giggled. *"If anyone else is there, then that's just a fortunate coincidence."*

Zaynab stared at the brick building with a row of large, white garage doors. "We both know I can just wait to show her when I go to iftar at her house tonight." She let her head drop on the steering wheel. "How much more obvious and desperate can I be?"

"No more obvious than him, from what I've heard."

"Yeah." Zaynab closed her eyes and let Xander's face materialize. His diamond cheeks over his brown, groomed beard filled the blackness of her lids. One corner of his mouth lifted just a little higher than the other into a sexy smile that made her melt. She first noticed it when he and Mansur started eating at the other end of the dining table. Every night for weeks, she would try to get him to treat her to one. They became more frequent with each evening. "Still, making an excuse to chat him up at his job isn't the most Islamic thing."

"*I can't think of anything more Islamic than finding a spouse to complete half your faith.*"

A cop car parked next to Zaynab. "So, is that the story we're going with?" She offered the blond police officer in the drive seat a wave. He nodded and got out.

"*It's not a story,*" Sabrina said. "*You don't have to be one of those shrinking violet women who waits for a man to decide he wants to marry her.*"

"I will not ask him to marry me."

"*Why not? It's perfectly fine for a Muslim woman to let a man know she may want to marry him.*"

Zaynab grabbed her handbag from the passenger seat and picked up her cell phone. "Well, I'm not one of them. I'm just adjusting to the idea of marrying again. It's bad enough I'm coming here, not even knowing if he is here."

"*I don't blame you. I wouldn't be able to do it either. Hold on. He might not be there?*" Sabrina's hearty laughter blasted through the phone. "Sis, *you're a mess.*"

"I know. Gotta go. Salams." Zaynab hung up and followed the officer. He strutted up the building walkway with a gait of confidence she longed to have. Truth? It scared her to death that what she perceived as signals from Xander were merely him being nice. How big a fool would she be then? No. She wasn't that clueless and knew when a man was into her. There had been enough of them during her travels. She walked through the glass doors and stopped at the reception counter. "Hi. I'm here to see Faiza Salih. My name is Zaynab."

"Hi," said the man in a crisp white shirt on the other side of the glass. "She's expecting you." He pointed at a big metal door. "Just go through there."

Zaynab passed through the door, stepping onto the gray

concrete. She scanned the rows of fire trucks. "Faiza?" she called out.

Faiza appeared from behind a truck, rushing toward her in a pair of turnout pants and a long-sleeve tee. She gave Zaynab salams and a hug. "I'm so glad you came here with your new car." She put an arm around Zaynab's back. "Now, we can go for a drive without the kids."

Zaynab craned her neck, searching the station. "Yeah, I know, right?" She heard a noise and looked over her shoulder. A man hoisted a blue bag with the Star of Life emergency medical logo on it.

"He isn't here."

Zaynab faced Faiza, lifting her chin. "Who's not here?"

Faiza shook her head and slowly blinked. "Xander."

"Why would I be looking for Xander?"

Faiza dropped her arm and walked ahead. "Because you've started your own little fire for him for weeks."

Zaynab shuffled quickly behind her. "A fire? Really? That's the best you can do."

"It's accurate."

"No, it's corny."

Faiza leaned her head back. "Ha! It's not as corny as the two of you have been at my dining table." She stopped and spun around. "Are you going to deny it?"

Zaynab pressed her lips. Faiza was way too perceptive for her to deny anything. "No."

A triumphant grin spread over Faiza's face. "Good. Like you could anyway." She resumed her cocky exit out of the station. "I think it's good that you're interested in someone, and you picked a good one with Xander."

Zaynab frowned and clicked the key fob. "You're that sure, huh?"

Faiza stopped on the passenger side and looked over the car's roof. "I'm that sure."

Zaynab swung the door open. "Well, before you have me signing any contracts, how about I get to know him better?" She started to climb inside.

"Fine, right after you get intended. Mansur said he's sure Xander will ask soon."

Zaynab snapped straight. "What? Ar-are you serious?" They got in.

"Yes—" she clicked the buckle "—now, let's give this baby a spin."

Zaynab sat behind the wheel, just as motionless as when she was in the accident. The world spun in front of her. She crushed on Xander, but was she ready for a husband? The last year of life with Mansur flashed in front of her.

Faiza touched her arm. "You okay?"

Zaynab flinched. "Huh? Yeah. I don't know if this is the right time for courtship. I barely got my act together, and things with Beni are going well."

"It's a perfect time. Don't hide behind your son or condition. Beni is fine, and you have your anxiety under control. Let things take their course with Xander. If nothing comes out of it, at least enjoy the attention."

Zaynab started the car. Things would not be the same with Xander. Unlike Mansur, he was her choice. She wanted to get closer to him. "You're right." The car's engine hummed. She put it into reverse and backed out of the parking stall. "Let's see what happens."

14

NEW JOB

Zaynab crossed her legs, stopping them from shaking and her heels from making a clacking sound on the industrial tile floor. Nothing was more exciting or terrifying than starting something new. This Ramadan had a lot of new things to make her jumpy. First Xander and now a job.

She took measured breaths into her nose and out her slightly open lips. *You can do this. It's in Allah's hands.* She closed her eyes and let the sound of clicking keyboards from the desks on the other side of the counter soothe her. It took every mental tool she had to resist the instinct to bolt out of the school's office. She couldn't afford to leave, anyway. The savings from her old job she quit after having Beni were more than half gone. She spent it and whatever part of her dowry from Mansur that wasn't tied up in investments. An additional stream of income was essential if she wanted to stay independent.

She glanced at the closed office door with the word *Principal* in golden letters. The interview went well. She must've made a good impression because they asked her to return for a second one. Her heart jumped when it swung open.

"Zaynab?" The school principal, Sister Bathory, motioned for her to come. "As-salam alaykum, we're ready for you." Zaynab followed Sister Bathory into the large office lined with ceiling-high shelves filled with books on every wall. "Please, have a seat."

She sat next to the assistant principal, Brother Martinez, and smiled. "Thank you for asking me back."

"You're welcome. Sister Bathory flipped through a stack of papers on her desk. "We think you'll be an excellent addition to our staff."

The rest of the meeting went by in a blur. Sister Bathory handed her a ton of forms to complete and ushered her to the main office's exit just as the bell rung and students flooded the hallway. She tucked the papers under her arm and meandered through the crowd of children, pulling out her phone and selecting a new number in her contacts list—Xander's. He gave it to her the night before, requesting that she call him as soon as she found out if they hired her. Flutters ran through her stomach with each ring.

His husky voice came through the phone. He gave salams. *"How did it go?"*

She side-stepped a group of girls in navy abaya uniforms and white hijabs. "Alhamdulillah. I got the job."

"I knew you would. When do you start?"

"Monday. I have three days to complete a ton of forms they gave me." She exited the school. The sunny day warmed her, along with the thrill surging through her from the blessings showered on her.

"I'm sure you'll get it done. They're lucky to have you."

She dug her keys from her purse, crossing the parking lot. "Yes, they are."

"Listen," he said, his tone changing to one more stoic. "We've been talking for weeks now."

She stopped. "Yes." She held her breath to the silence.

"I want more. It's torture sitting across from you every night and trying to keep things platonic."

She snickered, trying to seem relaxed despite the inward storm stirring. "That's a big word. You must be serious."

"I am. Everything you do fans a flame in me. I see you do something as simple as lick your lips, and it's all I can do to stop from taking them with mine. I know I'm being forward, which is why I'm sure that it's time for us to be intended. What do you think?"

She swallowed the lump in her throat. "I—" she jumped and shrieked at a loud honk. A line of cars, filled with irritated drivers, had formed behind her. "Oh, I'm sorry." She scurried out of their way.

"What's happening?"

"Nothing. Everything's fine. You want to get intended?"

"I spoke to Mansur about introducing me to your father."

"You did?"

"I'm ready for us to talk about a future together. Are you?"

She rubbed at the turbulence swelling in her gut. It was a good feeling, stemming from the anticipation of their acquaintance turning into something more. "Yes, I am."

Xander let out a sigh of relief. "*Alhamdulillah*. Mansur said your father is in seclusion for the last ten days of Ramadan."

"Yes, he tries to do it every year."

"*Mansur is arranging for us to meet at the masjid for iftar tomorrow night.*"

"So soon?" she croaked through her closing throat.

"*Do you need more time?*"

"No, no. I'll go to the masjid for iftar tomorrow night too." She let out a nervous giggle. "You're not playing."

"No, I'm not. I won't be at dinner tonight. I'm going to my parents' house."

"Oh, okay." She masked the disappointment pricking her from her voice.

"I'll see you at the masjid tomorrow night?"

"Alright. Hey, Faiza and I are taking the kids to the aquarium tomorrow. Why don't you come?" She slammed her eyes shut. Five minutes hadn't passed since the man asked about marrying her, and she was cornering him into a family outing.

"I'd like that. Text me the time and directions. I'll meet you guys there."

Her stomach somersaulted. "I will." She gave salams and hung up. "Well, I guess it's on." She got into the car and dropped the papers next to her and left the school with a new job and fiancé.

A tumultuous mix of excitement and panic raged inside her the entire ride home. She was ready to explore a relationship with Xander but not for the potential drama that may come from her parents. Ever since her divorce, she dodged their attempts to arrange another marriage for her. After a litany of arguments about her refusing any suitor they presented, how was she going to let them know she found someone on her own?

∼

Zaynab pulled into the driveway behind Om's Mercedes. Abo's car would be gone for the rest of Ramadan. Ali's car wasn't there either. He bolted out of town exactly two weeks after Ramadan began.

She got out with the papers and strode into the house, nerves jumping. "As-salam alaykum!" she called out after entering. She rushed up the staircase, hoping no one had heard her. At the top of the steps, she turned and looked down. No response. *Om must be sleeping.* She crept through the house, noting the lack of aroma from her mother's cooking. With Abo at the masjid and her and Ali gone, Om hadn't reason to make any big meals. *I should stay with her. She shouldn't have to eat alone.* She took out her phone from her purse and pulled up Faiza's number. Nerves of resistance crackled through her. She wanted to see Beni so much. Missing dinner with him would be torture. She put the phone away and tiptoed to her parents' bedroom door, cracking it open and peeking inside. Om lay in the center of the bed. Steady breathing from her slumber filled the room. Zaynab sighed and closed the door before rushing to the bedroom. She closed the door with a soft click, putting off any conversation about Xander. What a chicken.

15

THE WAY WE DO IT

"You're getting married?!" Ma dropped the pencil and puzzle book and sat straight. She folded her arms over her lap and glared across the sectional at Xander with a look that demanded answers. It had been a nice evening. Ma cooked an exceptional dinner, and they caught up on the past few weeks. The news of his plans to marry Zaynab would end all the Heath family fun. Ma appeared poised to argue. Dad kept his eyes on the TV with his feet up on the Ottoman, wiggling his toes like he hadn't a care in the world.

Xander leaned his elbows on his spread legs, knowing that the explanation he had for them wouldn't be good enough for Ma. "I'm planning on it. I've met someone."

Ma's eyes narrowed. "Someone?"

"Yes. Her name is Zaynab."

"Zaynab? What about Violet?"

Xander grunted and stood, picking up his empty glass. "Why would it be Violet?"

Ma followed him into the hall, little feet stomping on the floor. "Because she's your fiancé."

He stopped and turned. "*Was* my fiancé."

"She can be again."

The hope twinkling in Ma's eyes filled him with apprehension. What did he have to do to get her to let go of the possibility of him reuniting with Violet? He leaned on one leg. "No, she can't." He sighed and stroked her arm. "Look, Ma, I'm interested in someone else."

Ma sucked her teeth and pushed his hand away. "Just like that? You're out of love with Violet and in love with this Zay-whoever?"

"No." He shoved a hand in his back pocket. "Look, Ma. It took me a while to move on from my relationship with Violet, but that's what I've done. You need to accept it."

"How long have you known this woman?"

"A few weeks."

"And you're ready to marry her? Not dating or anything?"

"I'm not marrying her tomorrow. After I go to the mosque tomorrow night and talk with her father, we're going to court for a while and see how it goes. We're Muslim. That's the way we do things."

"Get out of the boy's love life, Lydia!" Dad hollered from the den.

"Shut up, Frank!" Ma yelled over her shoulder. She held out her hand. "Give me that."

Xander passed his mother the glass and went to the steps. "I'm going to wash up and go to the masjid for prayer."

Ma sighed and shuffled back into the den. "*You know, Frank, you could take a little more interest in your son's life.*"

"*He's fine and grown. He'll do what he wants.*"

Xander rushed up the stairs, and into his old bedroom, closing the door to his parents' bickering. He passed remnants of his youth as he entered the bathroom. The tile floors sent a cool rush up his legs. He stood in front of the white porcelain sink and turned on the faucet, letting the water run. He held his fingers under the icy stream, waiting for it to warm up. This would be the first Ramadan night he spent at the old masjid since he moved away. It might be nice if he saw some brothers he met when he was first Muslim. Although, he would miss an evening with Zaynab, Beni, Mansur and Faiza.

He washed for prayer before jogging back downstairs and into the kitchen. Ma leaned on the island counter on the phone, her back to him.

"You need to do something before—" she stopped talking and turned "—um the milk curdles. Let me know how it turns out. Bye." She hung up. Her lips turned into a nervous grin. More like guilty.

Xander squinted at her. "Who was that?"

She chuckled. "Jennifer. She's making rice pudding. Are you coming back?"

He jerked the refrigerator door open. "Yeah. I don't have to work tonight, so I'll sleep here. I'm going to be up early for the pre-fast meal." He searched the inside of the fridge.

"How about I wrap you a plate of leftovers? Then, all you have to do is heat it up in the microwave."

He closed the refrigerator and faced his mother. "That would be great. Thanks." He pecked her cheek. "I'll be back late."

"Alright, sweetie."

He glanced back at her. Sweetie? What was she up to? He made his way out of the house, deciding that it was better to leave it alone and concentrate on getting to prayer. The night air embraced him. He gazed past the trees at the constellations in the sky. Peace surrounded him before he got into his truck and drove to the masjid.

∽

Xander stopped the truck and grunted at the sight of the packed parking lot. He had left his parents' house late, leaving him to search for a space. He pressed the gas. There was no place to park in the lot, so he kept driving, passing cars parked along the streets. He craned his neck back and forth, not stopping until he spotted a space two blocks away. Parallel parking between a sports car and minivan took a while. By the time he hopped out and jogged to the masjid, people poured out of the entrance. "Aw, man!" He stopped and gulped for air. After looking at his watch, he caught his breath. Isha prayer was over, but he could make the last one. All wasn't lost. He strolled toward the building and put a foot on the first step leading to the brothers' entrance.

"Xander!" someone shouted from the other side of the masjid. "Xander! Wait!"

The familiar voice and clicking of heels on the pavement tapped Xander's nerves. He clenched his teeth and looked over the crowd of heads turned in the voice's direction. His gaze met Violet's. A scarf, loosely draped over her head, flapped in the breeze as she raced toward him.

She stopped in front of him, holding a hand to her chest. "There you are. They told me to wait by the women's door for you. What's the deal with that? Women have a separate entrance?"

He looked around them and then peered at her. "What are you doing here?"

"I told you I was interested in becoming Moozlem. Remember?"

"Mus-lim." He studied her face, beautiful and manipulative. True, he gave her the masjid information, so she could investigate Islam, but how had she known he'd be here to wait for him? His mother on the phone came to the forefront of his mind. He stiffened his back and rubbed his beard. "I remember. Have you learned anything? How long have you been coming here? Have you met anyone?"

Violet's eyes widened. She blinked and shifted her gaze. "What's with all the questions?"

He grunted and squinted at her. "You didn't know there's a separate entrance for sisters. This is your first time here, isn't it?"

"So, what if it is?"

He climbed the now empty stairs. "Good night, Violet. The next prayer is about to start."

She rushed up the stairs and blocked him. "Wait. You're going to turn me away from Islam?"

"I'm not turning you away." He waved an arm in the air. "You can learn about it from anyone here."

"Including you?"

"No, not including me." He moved to the side and continued up the steps. "I told you before, even if you become Muslim, we're over. You need to move on. I have."

"So, I've heard," she said in a snide tone. "Do you really think you can forget about what we had? Xander!"

He ignored her. Xander went through the men's entrance and pulled off his boots. He was moving forward with Zaynab.

16

AQUARIUM

"Mommy Zay, look!" Beni pressed his little hands against the glass. His eyes were as big as saucers. He moved his head back and forth, as if he was trying not to miss anything in front of him.

Zaynab bent behind him and held him close with one arm. She pulled him away from the aquarium glass and put her head next to his. "No touching." The odor of chlorine fused with the scent of chocolate and sweat emanated from Beni. It took a lot of chasing the toddler around, but she had wiped most of the ice cream from his hands and face. A little was still stuck to the corners of his smiling mouth. She pointed at a hammerhead shark swimming toward them. "Do you see that one?"

"Yes, Mommy Zay!"

Alhamdulillah, they spent a wonderful afternoon together. Beni stayed stuck to her side, holding her hand and jumping in her arms. He came running to her every time she called out to him and showed more affection than ever, kissing her cheek and hugging her. She felt like a real mom again.

Xander sauntered up and stood next to them. He looked so fine in his snug tee shirt and jeans. His tattoos bulged under his arm muscles, and his smile as he gazed down at them took her breath away. It took all her self-control not to reach up and kiss him. "Had enough?" she asked as she rose and held Beni on a hip.

"Not at all," Xander said. He mussed Beni's soft curls with a brawny hand. "I'm having a great time. What's next?"

Zaynab searched the crowd. "We need to find Faiza. I think it's almost time to go. Maghrib is in a couple of hours."

Xander rubbed his abdomen. "Yeah, and I worked up an appetite running after this little man here."

Beni reached for Xander. "Make me a tree, 'Ander."

Xander laughed and hoisted Beni on his shoulders. "Let's go. I think she's still where we stopped to feed the kids."

Zaynab lumbered next to Xander. Her son's little feet dangled over his chest. He was incredible with Beni. He hadn't missed a beat all afternoon. They went to the food court. She spotted Faiza sitting in a corner with a receiving blanket draped over her shoulder. "There she is." They crossed the room, winding through round dining tables and chairs full of people. Zaynab sat next to her. She squeezed one of Bushra's tiny feet. "Salams. She still nursing?" Xander sat on the table's far side and propped Beni in his lap.

Faiza covered her yawning mouth. "Yes. I don't know why, but she is extra hungry today. Do you mind if we leave once, she's finished?"

"Absolutely," Zaynab said. "You've been great, coming out with two babies."

"It's fine." Faiza peeked under the blanket and smiled when Bushra's foot flicked back and forth. "I think she's almost done, finally."

Zaynab got up and hooked the diaper bag over her shoulder. "Why don't I bring the car to the front? We parked pretty far."

"That sounds good." Faiza stuck a hand under the blanket. "I'll get this one ready for the car ride."

Xander got up with Beni. "I'll go with you."

Zaynab couldn't keep the silly grin off her face or stop herself from batting her lashes. "Okay." It was as if Xander's name branded each of the butterflies scrambling inside her as he trailed behind her. She became more jittery the further they got from the aquarium. The feelings surging through her for Xander became too intense for her to handle. She let out an ungraceful chortle. "Did you smell all the food? I can't wait until iftar tonight."

"Me neither," Xander said behind her, "but not for the food." He moved next to her and tilted his head. "I can't wait to meet your father. I guess you haven't been able to talk to him about me, since he's in seclusion at the masjid."

"Um, no." She avoided direct eye contact. "Where is that car?" She pressed the key fob. The Jeep honked and its lights flashed. "There it is." She quickened her pace. The fluttering inside her gut went from butterflies to hornets that buzzed and made her chest tighten. She stopped at Faiza's car and propped her head on the cold driver's door glass, trying to control her panting.

Xander leaned against the car. "Are you okay?"

She stared at the pavement. "I will be," she said, breathless.

"Just breathe," he said with a calmness that chipped at the anxiety. "Take your time. Everything is alright."

Once her panting slowed to steady breathing, she lifted her head and looked at them. Beni's head lay on Xander's shoulder, his face turned away. She couldn't see how her panic attack affected him. She saw it on Xander's, his eyes filled with compassion. Or was it pity? He patted Beni's back and swayed. "Feeling better?"

She swallowed the knot in her throat. "Yes. I had an anxiety attack."

"I know."

She backed away from the car and looked down, fidgeting with the key fob. "I don't know if this is a good idea, Xander."

"What?"

"Us talking, courting." She grunted and shifted her weight. "I'm not perfect."

"None of us are."

She met his gaze. "I come with attachments and issues. I'm divorced with a son."

He widened his eyes and huffed in exaggerated disbelief. "You're kidding." He glanced at Beni. "So that's what this is on my chest, a kid?"

She walked to the trunk of the car. "Fine, be funny." She opened it and threw the diaper bag inside. "I also have Generalized Anxiety Disorder. There is no cure. It won't go away."

He opened the back door. "I get that, and I'm fine with it." He put Beni in his car seat. After buckling him in, Xander stood and faced her. "I have a past too."

"Like what?" She closed the distance between them.

"I was engaged before I became Muslim. After I took my Shahadah, the relationship fell apart."

"Are you still in love with her?" What a dumb question. She searched his face.

"No. I've moved on, but she's still trying to get back together."

She pinned her shoulders back. "I see." She jerked the driver's door open. "Well, if there is a chance of you getting back with your ex—"

"There isn't." Xander grasped the door, cornering her

between it and the car. "I want you." He bent closer to her. "Now, I'm going to talk to your father, and we're going to ask each other all the tough questions and plan our wedding. Understand?"

She let out a staggered breath and nodded, dizzy from the power and passion radiating from him to her. "Yes, Xander."

He stood straight. "Good. Take the car to Faiza—" he backed away from her "—I'm going to get ready for tonight." He poked his head in the car and gave Beni salams before strutting away.

Zaynab got into the car and looked at Beni through the rearview mirror. "Everything will to be fine, inshallah."

17

GET READY

"*B*ismillah." Xander bit into the spicy fritter filled with vegetables. He chewed, but the tension running through him made it tough to swallow despite his hunger. He scanned the brothers' dining hall for any sign of Mansur. No such luck. He slumped his shoulders and sipped from the water bottle. Where was he?

Xander shoved the rest of the fritter into his mouth. The few hours since he left Zaynab and Beni at the aquarium crept by like decades, not from his famished state but because of the excitement that he was going to make her his intended. He hadn't felt this sure or exhilarated since the day he became Muslim.

"You're quiet tonight," a Nigerian brother sitting next to him said. He gave Xander a friendly nudge with his elbow.

Xander scratched the back of his head. He hadn't been to the masjid for iftar since he started going to Mansur's house. He was not acquainted enough with the men surrounding him to share his life. "Yeah," he said, lifting his chin and resuming his search.

Mansur rushed into the dining hall and stopped in the middle of the room, turning as he looked around.

Xander shot up and waved. "Salams! Over here." He ignored the oglers and focused on Mansur, striding toward him. He hugged Mansur before they sat at the table.

"Sorry, I'm late, man." Mansur stretched an arm across the table and took one of the sealed water bottles in the middle. "It's difficult getting a wife and kids into the car. I didn't even break my fast yet." He took a swig.

"It's okay." Xander said. "I'm just glad you made it."

Mansur propped an elbow on the table. "I wouldn't miss it. I think you and Zaynab will be good together." He raised out of his seat a little and lifted his chin, squinting. "I don't see Fahad. He may have gone back down for prayer." On cue, the call to prayer echoed through the room. "Yeah. He's probably down there already. I'll introduce you to him during dinner."

Xander stood with all the other men in the room. "Sounds good." They poured out of the dining hall and descended the stairs. His phone buzzed. He read a message from Zaynab.

Zaynab: *Salams. I'm here.*

He tucked the phone in his pocket. It wouldn't be long before Zaynab was his to cherish.

~

Zaynab turned her head from right to left, closing the evening prayer. She lifted her cupped hands near her face and muttered a supplication for her and Xander. Tonight, would be the night that they came together.

She still hadn't the nerve to talk to her family about getting engaged. When she arrived home after the aquarium yesterday, she scurried—like a coward—to her room and changed. She left for Faiza's house before Om got up from her nap and returned late, so they barely talked before Zaynab flopped into bed, exhausted. They got up and ate Suhoor in relative silence. When Om approached her before she left for the masjid iftar later that day, Zaynab stuck to basic conversation with no mention of the sexy firefighter who stole her heart. The clueless smile on Om's face as she left strapped Zaynab with guilt, but not enough to let her mother in on the recent development.

Zaynab passed her palms over her face and stuck out her arm just in time to catch Beni, who had got up and was ready to create a ruckus with the rest of the children running over the ornate prayer carpet. "Oh, no you don't." She tickled his tummy. He bent over in a hysterical giggle.

"Good catch," Faiza said, smiling at them. She picked up Bushra and rose with a grunt. "I hope there is enough food. Nursing while fasting is no joke."

"I bet." Zaynab got to her feet and took Beni's hand. They made their way through the crowd of Muslim women in beautiful outfits, chatting. Once in the sisters' dining hall, they stood on the long, winding buffet line. Zaynab sighed. Jockeying for food at iftar never thrilled her, which is why she and her family rarely attended community meals during Ramadan. Xander was worth it, though.

Once they had braved the line of hungry fasters and piled their plates, Zaynab and Faiza stood next to each other in front of the dining tables. "Where should we sit?"

Faiza, balancing a plate in her free hand while holding Bushra, jutted her chin toward a table, empty save one woman sitting at it. "How about there?" The woman shifted in her seat, looking like a lost puppy. Women filled the surrounding tables, devouring their food. Some blatantly stared at the lone woman, probably feeding her obvious discomfort. "It looks like she's by herself."

Zaynab smirked. "And you can't have that, can you?"

"Nope. Let's go." They put their plates on the table and sat. "As-salam alaykum." Faiza offered the woman her right hand.

The woman stared at Faiza's hand with her doe-like brown eyes and batted her lashes as her peach lips pulled into a nervous smile. "Oh, hello. I'm Violet."

"Nice to meet you, Violet. I'm Faiza, and this is Zaynab."

Violet cast Zaynab a strange look. "Your name is Zaynab?"

"Yes. Do we know each other?"

Violet giggled. "I don't think so."

Faiza picked up her fork. "Is this your first time here?"

Violet adjusted the scarf draped over her head. "Um, yes. I'm not Muslim, but I am interested."

Zaynab put Beni on the chair next to her. "That's wonderful." She ripped off a piece of naan bread and handed it to him. "Have you been learning about it for long?"

Violet turned her heart-shaped face to Zaynab. "Not long. I started going to my local mosque a few weeks ago when Ramadan began."

"So, you don't live around here?" Faiza asked between bites.

"No. I live in the next county. But my fiancé lives here and goes to this one. He's a firefighter and moved here for his job."

Faiza's mouth dropped open. "A firefighter? I'm a firefighter too. What's your fiancé's name?"

"Xander Heath."

Zaynab's muscles clenched. She stared at Faiza. Xander's words at the aquarium flooded her mind.

I've moved on, but she's still trying to get back together.

She stood and picked up Beni, who protested being torn

away from the plate of food. "I'm sorry. You'll have to excuse me."

"Actually—" Faiza got up with Bushra in her arms "—excuse *us*."

Zaynab stormed out of the dining hall with her son, best friend, and one fussy baby.

18

BEDLAM

Xander thanked the server standing on the other side of the long buffet table. The man smiled and plopped a healthy portion of rice on the plate. Spicy smells from the array of food drifted into Xander's nose and mixed with the prickly sensation jolting through him. This level of nervousness rarely hit him. It hadn't been this way when he got engaged to Violet, but Zaynab was different.

Xander carried his plate to the center of the hall and searched for Mansur over a sea of heads bent over plates.

"Xander!" He caught sight of his friend standing at a packed table and waving. Mansur left the table, closing the distance between them. "Hey, it's about time you got off that line." He let out a chuckle. "Good news. I already talked to Fahad about you. He isn't keen on talking contracts or anything until after he's finished his seclusion, but he's willing to meet you."

"Alhamdulillah."

"I hope you're ready." Mansur gave Xander's back a gentle slap. "Let's go." He strode back to the table full of men, one of whom was Zaynab's father.

Xander followed, excitement swelling in his chest. Uneasiness seeped in with it as they got closer. He surveyed all the faces. Their laughter ceasing and smiles turning into an array of pressed lips and frowns as they settled their gazes on him. *Okay. The typical looks. I can handle it.* Normally, he wouldn't allow the glowers to faze him, but one of them was Zaynab's father, a man who held his happiness in his hands. They reached the table. Xander made eye contact with a man whose expression bore through him.

It was the same man who argued with him about his tattoos at the beginning of Ramadan. *Oh, Allah. Please don't let it be him.* Mansur prodded Xander by pressing between his shoulder blades. They stood in front of the man. *Aww, crap. It is him.*

Mansur raised a hand toward the man. "Fahad—" he put the same hand to his chest "—this is Xander Heath. He's interested in—"

Fahad shot up; eyes narrow with rage. "La!" he shouted the Arabic word for no and slammed a fist on the table. The entire hall grew quiet. All eyes on the furious man. He glared at Mansur. "How dare you bring this *shaqs ajeeb* to me about my daughter?"

Mansur looked between Fahad and Xander in disbelief, then cleared his throat. "Xander is not a weirdo. He's a good man who wants—"

"I don't care what he wants! Look at him!" Fahad screwed his face with disgust as Arabic flowed from his mouth.

Xander couldn't understand the man, but Fahad's disapproval for him came through in the vileness of his tone. Anyone around them who spoke Arabic either gave Xander a look of contempt or pity. Both tore at him. He lifted his chin and set his jaw. Mansur answered Fahad in the language, pointing at the tattoos peeking from Xander's collar and on his hands. Soon, the two of them went back and forth with increasing animosity. Xander raised his palms. "Enough!" The room settled again, and everyone stared at him. He met Fahad's gaze. "Brother, you don't even know me."

Fahad scoffed. "I don't want to know you, and I won't allow you to come near Zaynab."

Xander crossed his arms. "That's too bad, because I plan on courting your daughter. We care for each other."

Fahad sniggered. "Care for each other? I don't believe you. Zaynab wouldn't give someone like you the time of day." He jabbed a finger at Xander as he spoke. "If you think she'll get engaged without my permission, you're crazy. She knows to respect and obey her father."

"Which is why I asked Mansur to introduce us," Xander said.

"Well, you've wasted your time." Fahad sat back in his seat. "Now, go. You've ruined enough of my meal and seclusion." He stabbed at a piece of meat with the same precision that his rejection stabbed at Xander's heart.

Xander went to walk around the table. The situation was not hopeless. He would have Zaynab.

Mansur grasped Xander's shoulder, stopping him. He slowly shook his head before turning it toward Fahad. "Listen to reason, Fahad."

Fahad continued to eat as if he was the only person in the room.

Xander's phone buzzed in his pocket. He took it out and read the screen.

Zaynab: *Come down now. I need to speak to you.*

Mansur's phone beeped at the same time. "It's Faiza," he said, frowning down at the device. "She wants us downstairs now. I wonder what's going on?"

Xander glanced at Fahad before dropping his plate on the table. "We might as well go find out."

~

*X*ander remained still at the top of the steps, controlling his breathing. Years of disaster training fortified him and prevented him from blowing his cool. However, he struggled to stay calm despite his experience and ability to deescalate the tensest situations. His meeting with Fahad was a train wreck. Now he watched Zaynab pace at the bottom of the steps. Light from the masjid floodlights shone on her strained face. She was clearly upset. How would she react when he told her about Fahad rejecting him? One thing at a time. He had to find out what made her agitated.

"Salams." Xander crept down the stairs. Mansur followed.

Zaynab ceased her pacing, standing next to Faiza, who held Bushra on a hip and had a firm grasp of Beni's hand. Both women peered at him like inquisitors ready to strap him to a stake. "Everything okay?"

Zaynab put her hands on her hips. "Do you know someone named Violet?"

Xander slammed his eyes shut and groaned. Violet couldn't be here. One only found this much drama on television shows. "Yes. She's my ex-fiancé. I told you about her earlier."

"Yes, you did." The ire in Zaynab's voice was almost the same as her father's. "Well, she's here, and she doesn't have the *ex*-part down. She's claiming that you *are* her fiancé."

Xander raised and dropped his arms, slapping the sides of his legs. He let out a groan while gazing at the starry sky. *Ya, Allah. Could this night get any worse?*

"Xander?" Violet's voice reached him and plucked his last shred of patience. She shot Zaynab a wary look before approaching him with her arms open. "Is everything okay?"

He raised his hands in front of himself, moving away from her. "What are you doing here?"

She stepped closer; her lips pursed in a coy smile. "I'm here to see you." She put a hand on his chest.

Xander cringed and pushed her hand away. Many would probably think her touching him was not a big deal, but to those gawking at them in front of the masjid, Violet made a gesture of public affection for a man who was not her husband. "Violet, stop. You're not here to see me." He turned to Zaynab, who stared, bewildered. Only what she thought mattered. He had to clear up this mess. "I can explain."

"No," Zaynab said, glowering at Violet. Ever since the woman announced that she was Xander's fiancé, rage boiled within her. Violet was playing games and was about to lose. "I get what's happening." She faced Faiza. "I think you should go back inside with the children."

"Yeah, right," Faiza said, putting Bushra in Mansur's arms before crossing her own. "I'm not going anywhere."

Zaynab searched her friend's face. They didn't have to say anything to each other. It was clear as day that Faiza had her back, which only fed her determination to make quick work of Violet. She stepped between Xander and his ex, peering at the petite woman. "Violet, is it? You're obviously mistaken about any engagement to Xander."

Violet sneered and tilted her head, dragging her gaze up Zaynab's body. "And who the hell are you?"

Zaynab pinned her shoulders back and lifted her chin. She inched closer to Violet. Faiza moved behind her. "I'm the one telling you that Xander isn't for you. So, if he's why you're here, you need to leave." Adrenalin surged through her.

Violet's white face reddened. She glared at Zaynab. "Or what?"

Zaynab clenched her fists. "Or there'll be a problem." Was she ready to fight in the middle of the masjid parking lot over Xander? Yes.

Violet leaned to one side, squinting at Xander. "Is this who Lydia was talking about, Xander?"

"Yes," Xander said. Was that a hint of pride in his tone? "Look, Violet. It's been over between us for a long time. I don't know why you can't get that, but you need to stop going to my parents' house and following me around."

"But—" Violet stepped to the side. Zaynab and Faiza moved, blocking her. "Oh, come on."

"I told you," Zaynab snapped, "he's not for you."

"Xander," Violet pleaded.

"You should go," Faiza said, from behind Zaynab.

"But I fasted all day," Violet whined.

"Then go eat, but stay away from Xander," Zaynab warned.

Violet's eyes flashed. She rolled them and snorted. "How welcoming is this?" She turned on her heels and stormed across the parking lot, getting into a red car. It roared out of the lot and vanished into the night.

Zaynab kept her back facing Xander, not ready to see his response to her cocky claim on him. Had she lost her mind? No, Xander was for her, and she wouldn't let anybody come between them.

"Well," Mansur said with an underlying chuckle, "I expected some Ramadan drama, but not this." He belted out a laugh. "Imagine, my wife and ex-wife ready to throw down with my friend's ex-girlfriend during iftar. You can't make this stuff up."

Faiza poked Mansur's side, which only made him laugh harder. "You're a mess."

"Yeah, but I'm your mess." He kissed her nose. "Can we go eat now?"

"You guys go ahead," Xander said. "I need to talk to Zaynab." He walked to the front of her as Mansur and Faiza went back into the masjid with the kids.

Zaynab concentrated on his boots. All the bravado she had with Violet crumbled around them. "I hope you don't think I overstepped my bounds."

"Look at me." She raised her head. His eyes burned with an intensity that sent waves of desire into her. "Not at all."

"You're not appalled?"

"That you were ready to fight over me? No." He grinned and puffed up his chest like a peacock. "It made me feel special that you would defend my honor."

She shook her head. "Always a joke with you."

His expression grew serious. "I'm sorry you had to go through that."

She shrugged. "I've experienced worse than a jealous ex. Each of us has issues and drama, remember? If we get married, we'll work through them together, inshallah."

Xander sighed and straightened, staring at the masjid. "About that."

Her heart sank. Had he changed his mind about marrying her? "What is it?"

He dipped his head and shuffled his feet. "My meeting with your father didn't go well."

"What happened?"

"Zaynab!" Abo shouted. "Zaynab!" She spun, her chest tightening at the sight of Abo standing at the top of the stairs, his face twisted with rage. "Get away from him, now!"

19

WAKIL

Zaynab stared at Xander. "What's going on?"

Abo flew down the stairs and clamped onto Zaynab's arm. "I said to get away from him." He yanked her toward him. She tried to resist, but he was too strong.

She stumbled into his arms. "Abo, what is wrong with you?" She watched her father. His face, twisted in a scowl, burned red with rage. She felt his quaking fingers dig into her side. He was rarely so angry.

"What's wrong with you? First, you leave your husband, now you want to run after this *shaqs ajeeb*." Abo pinned her tight to his side and glared at Xander. A small crowd gathered around them. Mansur appeared at the top of the stares. He rolled his eyes toward the sky before ambling down the steps.

Zaynab pushed at Abo's chest. "Do you know Xander?"

"No, he doesn't know me," Xander said. His eyes smoldered with scorn as he spoke and glared at Abo. "He just stares at me, thinking he does."

Abo let go of Zaynab and pushed her behind him, closing

the distance between him and Xander. "I already told you. I don't want to know you."

"Listen, Fahad." Mansur wedged an arm between Xander and Abo. "You can't judge a man by sight only. Xander is a decent brother."

Abo turned to Mansur, his nostrils flaring. "I can't believe that you're defending him. Why are you trying to tie down my daughter, the mother of your son, to some degenerate?"

She tugged on her father's shoulder. "No, Abo. He's a good person."

"Yeah," Mansur said. "He works with Faiza at the station, and he's my friend."

Abo wouldn't budge or cease staring daggers at Mansur. "Do you think I care that he's your buddy?"

Zaynab kept pulling at his shoulder. "Listen, Abo."

"You stay out of this." He swept her hand away.

"Stay out of it?!" Zaynab bellowed. She stormed around her father and brought her face close to his. "It's my life!" she screeched in his face.

His eyes grew large, making her gut twist. He glanced around them. "Go home," he growled in her face. The scent of dinner lingered on his breath.

Largely, men surrounded them. Faiza wasn't there to back her, but she couldn't waiver, not now. She took a step back, shaking her head. "No, Abo." A few women around them gasped and men grumbled. What a mistake. To a bunch of Muslim men, her asserting herself appeared defiant and disobedient, striking at her father's male ego. She stiffened. Too late to care about what anyone thought now. "I'm staying, and you need to hear me."

Abo's arm shot out at her. She stumbled back, falling into Xander's arms. For the first time in her life, she feared her father. He never touched her roughly before, not even a spanking when she was little. "Abo!" she screamed.

He snatched his hand back with a shocked expression, as if stunned by his behavior.

"Brother Fahad!" Imam Jobe's voice came from the top of the steps. Everyone turned to him. He reached for Abo, settling a hand on his arm. "You must calm yourself." The words and the imam's tone coaxed away the tension and violence hovering around them. "Whatever is happening, it's not worth such strife between you and your daughter." Abo's shoulders slumped. A reassuring smile spread across the imam's face. He looked at Xander. "Come, let's all talk in my office. Sister, please join us."

Everyone moved away from her. She trailed behind Imam Jobe with Abo, Xander and Mansur following her. Once in the office, the imam pulled back a chair. "Here, sister," he said to Zaynab. He walked around the desk littered with papers and decorated with incense burners and a model of the Ka'ba. "Please tell me what has made you so upset, Brother Fahad." Imam Jobe sat.

Abo took a seat in the chair next to Zaynab. He dragged the chair close to the desk and propped an elbow on it. He explained everything to the imam while Xander and Mansur leaned on the wall behind them. She glanced back a few times to gauge Xander's expression. His lips pressed into a thin line. He hadn't looked at her once. Her heart wrenched at the thought that it may be over between them. She couldn't let Abo's stubbornness ruin what she found with Xander.

"Okay," Imam Jobe said, after Abo finished talking and settled in his seat. "Do you want to place intentions on the sister, Brother Xander?"

Xander straightened with his chest expanded. "I do."

The corners of Imam Jobe's mouth twitched as he shook his head like an elder amused by the audacity of a younger man. "And sister, are you interested in the brother?"

"Yes." Zaynab perched on the edge of the chair. "The only reason my father disapproves is because he hates Xander's tattoos. He doesn't know him like I do."

Imam Jobe raised his brows. "What is your acquaintance with the brother?"

"We met when he rescued me from a car wreck. He pulled me out and went to the hospital to make sure I was okay. I've gotten to know him because we both go to Mansur's house for iftar." She turned and pinned Xander's gaze. "He's kind and wise, and he's good with Beni." Her heart filled with admiration for him.

"It sounds like you've developed feelings for him," Imam Jobe said.

"I have." She faced Imam Jobe. "I want to get engaged to him."

Abo scoffed. "Well, I won't allow it, and you can't get married without me."

"Actually, I can." She turned to her father. "I need a wakil. It doesn't have to be you." All the men looked surprised. The words coming out of her mouth shocked her just as much as they stunned Abo and everyone else. She pinned her shoulders back. "I can ask Imam Jobe to advocate for me, since you can't see past your bigotry."

Abo jumped out of his seat and towered over her. "You wouldn't dare!"

Imam Jobe stretched an arm across the desk and pressed his palm on a stack of papers. "All right, let's settle down. Sister, your father is the best person to act on your behalf. He loves you and wants what's best for you."

Zaynab crossed her legs and gazed past Imam Jobe at the Quranic text hanging on the wall. "I don't know about that. I've found a good match, and he refuses to let me be happy."

"You're disobedient and ungrateful," Abo said.

She stood. "Disobedient? All I've ever done was listen to you."

"Zaynab," Xander said, standing in front of her. "I don't want to come between you and your family."

She resisted the urge to stroke his beard. "You're not. This isn't about you." She stepped past Xander and met her father's furious gaze. "I've always done what I was told. I married Mansur because you and Om wanted me to, and it almost destroyed me." She looked over her shoulder at Mansur. "No offense."

He chuckled. "None taken."

"I'm building a life for myself and making my own decisions. I'm going to find out if he's the man for me. You can respect that or not, but that's what's happening." She gave salams and strode out of the office, not stopping or breathing until she reached her car. The adhan blasted from the speakers bolted to the masjid's outer walls. She got in and pulled out of the parking lot, finally in the driver's seat.

∽

"*We made prayer, then I left.*" Xander's voice filled the inside of the car. "*Your father didn't say another word after you stormed out.*"

Zaynab popped the last bit of cheeseburger in her mouth and turned the corner. After leaving the masjid, she had stopped at a halal restaurant. With a filled stomach, she thought with a little more clarity, but wasn't ready to go home. She took the longest route possible. "Sorry about that."

"*No. I understand. Your father will never accept me.*"

"I doubt it, but that doesn't matter. I accept you."

"*I told you. I don't want to be the reason for a rift between you and your family.*"

She pulled to the side of the road and stopped. "And I told

you-you aren't. It was bound to happen. Remember when we talked about my divorce and me living in Kuwait?"

"Yeah."

"I didn't have to stay there for so long. I could've moved back months ago. Instead, I avoided my parents. So much about me changed. I found my voice and sorted out what I wanted out of life. I knew they weren't ready for the new me."

"So, chasing Violet away and standing up to your father is all new?"

She giggled, steering back into traffic. "Very much so."

"I'm glad I know the new Zaynab. I want her to be my wife."

"Don't worry, she will be, inshallah." She turned into the driveway behind her father's car. "Oh, boy. My father is home. He left his seclusion."

"Let me know how it goes."

"I will." She gave Xander salams and went into the house. "Salams," she called out, kicking off her shoes and inching further inside the dim entryway.

"I can't believe you grabbed her." Om's voice drifted from the kitchen. *"She's your daughter, Fahad."*

Zaynab crept to the kitchen doorway, not believing her ears. Om was defending her? She stopped at the entrance. Her mother stood over her father, who held his head in his palm, arm propped on the kitchen table.

"I know, *habibti*." Abo said in a pained voice. He ran his fingers through his hair. "I stopped myself. Ugh. I can't believe she's thinking of marrying that man."

The frown on Om's face softened. She massaged Abo's shoulders. "I don't know why you're surprised. She's her own woman now. We need to accept it or risk losing her. Do you want to never see her or our grandson?"

Abo groaned and reclined in the chair, tilting his head back and closing his eyes. "No, but that man—"

"Is who she wants to marry. I don't like it any more than you, but I'm at least ready to give him a chance. The more we fight it, the further she'll dig in." She kissed the tip of Abo's nose. "She gets that from you."

Zaynab cleared her throat and walked into the kitchen. She knelt next to Abo and smiled up at him. "I'm sorry."

He touched his forehead to hers. "Me too. So, you're in love with this man?" He stroked her back, allowing his fatherly love to overcome his anger.

"I care for him, yes."

His chuckle shook them. "It's more than that. You're willing to defy your father for him. You wouldn't do that for Mansur."

She met his gaze. "Then I guess it's love. I don't want Imam Jobe to be my wakil. I want you."

He cupped her cheek. His eyes glistened with tears. "You shall have me."

She threw her arms around his neck, sniffing from tears of joy. "Jazakallah."

"I'm glad that's settled." Om wiped her eyes and shuffled to the stove, picking up the kettle. "I'll make some tea, and you can tell us more about your *fiancé*."

Zaynab pulled out a chair. "Okay, Om." She took out her phone and messaged Xander.

Zaynab: *Salams. We're getting married*!

20

NEWLYWEDS

Streams of frankincense smoke floated around Zaynab. She closed her eyes and took a deep breath, squeezing her mother's hand in her right and Faiza's in her left. The three of them sat on the prayer carpet. Bushra's sleeping body lay in front of them. Her tiny chest rising and falling as Imam Jobe's voice came out of the speakers. He talked about the beauty of marriage, love, and a couple's dedication to one another. It was all beautiful but taking too long. She wanted to be alone with Xander already.

She lifted her lids. A few feet across from her, Xander sat on the carpet, facing the imam. He wore a white dress shirt and slacks, simple, just like her low-key champagne column wedding dress.

They decided against the stress of a huge wedding. She already had one when she married Mansur, and Xander remained firm in his determination that they don't offer the community any more spectacle—despite Om's disappointment. Xander and Mansur arranged for a wedding after the Isha prayer, and everyone had left.

Xander turned and winked at her. His expressions of

affection grew bolder with each passing day of their engagement, not that there were many. Neither of them could wait to marry. It took only a few weeks for each of them to complete their part of the marriage contract. They spent the rest of the Ramadan nights at her parents table talking, negotiating and falling deeper in love.

Abo tapped Xander's shoulder and gave him a warning glance before smiling back at her. He snubbed Xander at the dining table for a while, ignoring him or grilling him mercilessly. Over time, Abo's disdain lessened, and he begrudgingly fulfilled his duties as her father and wakil.

Imam Jobe got up and walked to Zaynab and the women, contracts in hand. Beni followed, looking as cute as ever in a little suit. "Please sign, sister," Imam Jobe said to Zaynab, holding a pen up to her.

Beni took the pen and jumped on Zaynab. "Here, Mommy Zay." The entire room burst with laughter.

"Jazakallah, sweetie." She signed her name next to Xander's and studied the two signatures. Together, as they should be.

Imam Jobe barely announced their marriage when Xander sprang from his spot and crossed the room. "Let's go," he said, bending over Zaynab and offering her a bent arm. She hooked hers in his. He lifted her and encircled an arm around her waist. The first feel of his touch sent shock waves through her. It was definitely different than when he pulled her out of her father's wrecked car.

She stroked his soft beard with her fingertips, something she'd been wanting to do for weeks. "Okay, but first—"

"But first—" Om wedged and arm between them "—we need to take some pictures. I need something to show my friends I couldn't invite."

"Om," Zaynab said with a hint of irritation.

Xander cupped her face. "No, she's right." He grinned and

hugged Om's shoulders with one arm. "It would be a crime for me not to take a picture with my beautiful mother-in-law, and I have to give some to Ma."

Om let out a girlish giggle. Xander had her fully charmed. She became his biggest champion. "It's a shame your parents couldn't come."

Xander frowned. "I know." Although his mother was nice to Zaynab when they met, and even cut off relations with Violet, but Lydia refused to step foot inside a masjid. Xander —in equal stubbornness—refused to have their wedding anywhere else. He smiled down at them. "No worries. My parents and brothers and sisters will be at the *walimah* in a couple of weeks." He squeezed Om. "Along with all of your friends. Now, let's take these pictures."

"I know just the spot," Om said, walking away.

"Don't worry," Xander whispered in Zaynab's ear as they followed. "I have Faiza on duty. She'll get us out of here."

Everyone took out their phones, except Abo. Zaynab smiled until her jaws ached. She never felt more grateful than when Faiza stopped the picture taking and ushered them out of the masjid. Zaynab gave Beni a goodnight kiss and climbed into Xander's humongous truck and settled on the seat, waving at the smiling faces as he pulled out of the stall.

"Are you ready to go home, Mrs. Heath?" Xander took her hand in his and lay them on the console, steering with his free one. He stroked her above her wrist with his thumb.

She felt a flush of heat. "Most definitely."

21

SIDE CHAIR

Xander pushed the apartment's front door open. "Honey, we're home."

Zaynab groaned as she stepped onto the stoop and under the triangular awning. "I know I'm supposed to like the sound of that, but it's so corny."

"No, it's traditional. Now, let me carry you over the threshold." He bent.

She dodged his arms. "That's fine. I have two legs." She swung her hips as she past him, talking over her shoulder. "You already carried me, remember?"

He belted out a laugh and jiggled the key from the lock. "But that was a car accident. This would've been different."

"True, but I've already been here before for dinner with my parents. I was just here a couple of days ago to bring some of my things."

"Good points." He tossed the keys on the side table next to the smoky gray sectional sofa. "Now, do you remember what we talked about last night?" He sat on the arm of the couch and pulled at the strings of his dress shoes.

"I do." She kicked off her shoes and straightened them

against the light gray wall, next to a pair of black bunker gear boots with yellow patches at the ankles. "You want me to strip for you." She leaned against the wall, nerves jumping through her. He was so sexy.

He tugged at the buttons on his shirt. "That's not exactly what I said. I just told you not to spend a bunch of time getting into a nightgown or teddy." He shrugged out of the shirt. Tattoos decorated his arms and disappeared under his white tank undershirt. "All I could think about for the past month is watching you get out of all those clothes."

She shook her head. "That's stripping."

"If you want to call it that. You don't have to. I don't want you to be uncomfortable."

"Oh, trust me, I'm comfortable. I may have my anxieties but getting busy with you is not one of them."

"Good to know." He crossed the shag rug and sat in a side chair. "I'm your husband now. I get to see what others don't." He propped an elbow on the arm and pointed, eyes piercing with authority. "Show me. I want you to uncover every inch of your body that I've dreamed about seeing, touching, and tasting. The wait has been torture. Now I get to do everything to you I imagined as I lay alone in my bed at night." He leaned back and spread his legs. She stared at the bulge in his pants that was clearly obvious across the room. Less than an hour ago, she had to avoid too much direct eye contact with him. A tingle shot through her, making her folds throb in anticipation. She removed the pins from her hijab, trembling under his unwavering gaze. "Drop everything on the floor," he commanded with a sultry base in his tone. "Leave nothing on." She obeyed. The chiffon fabric cascaded to the floor along with the semblances of her inhibitions.

She loosened her hair from its bun and spread the tendrils over her shoulders. Then she reached back and undid the buttons to her dress and let it slide down her body until it crumpled next to the boots. "Is this what you've been thinking about, Xander?" She glided her fingertips down the front of the burgundy bra. Her nipples visible behind the see-through fabric.

"Exactly." He looked over her body and nodded. "Come here."

She strolled toward him, unclasping the bra, unashamed as she dropped it on the sofa and stood over him. "What now?"

He straightened and slid his palms up her thighs, gripping her buttocks. "You're sexier than I imagined." He nestled his nose between her legs and growled, sending vibrations right into her.

She gripped his shoulders, bracing herself under trembling legs. Xander buried his face further. The world spun. Coolness from her increasingly wet panties tickled her lower lips. It all felt way too good. "Xander, yes." She cupped the back of his head and tilted her hips forward. His moan showed that he knew exactly what he was doing to her. He tugged at the strings holding her panties on her hips, yanking them down her legs. She pushed his head back and crushed her lips to his and slid her tongue into his mouth. Traces of her juices passed between them. She deepened her kiss, wanting to taste more of him and herself.

He turned his head to one side and sat back. She pushed him against the back of the chair and straddled his legs. "More," she moaned before pulling his undershirt over his head. The tattoos across his chest mesmerized her. She traced the intricate floral and geometric patterns. His muscles quaked. She brushed her lips along the decorations, making a trail across his chest and up his neck.

He moaned, fueling the primal energy surging between them. She rubbed herself against the bulge in his pants. "That's it, babe. You want it, don't you?"

"Mmm," she moaned.

He held her hips and prompted her up. "And I'm ready to give you every inch of me until you scream." He muttered a prayer. He jerked open his pants and slid them down, revealing his stiffness, rock-hard and ready for her.

After repeating the same prayer, she jumped on it like a tigress in heat. He filled her as she sank onto his lap. The stretching ache stilled her for a moment. She dropped her head back and arched her back, taking in more of him. "Oh. I've wanted this so bad for so long." She swayed her hips back and forth.

He clamped down on them. "Don't move, not until I tell you." He cupped her breasts, teasing each nipple until they pebbled. He brought one to his lips, kissing it, then drawing it in and rolling it between the roof of his mouth and tongue. Her body burned with the urge to move on top of him. It raged higher with every kiss, suck, and pinch he treated her to.

"Xander, please. I-I want to…"

He looked up at her. "You want to what?" His question demanded an answer, the only one she could give him.

"I want to ride you, feel all of you until I burst."

He grabbed her buttocks with each hand. "Go ahead, babe. Do what you want."

She rolled her hips slowly, quickening as erotic fervor built inside her. Xander took over, guiding her until she bounced on his stiffness in a feverish cadence. Their thighs smacked together, creating a lustful rhythm accompanying their moans of pleasure. It had been a long time since she had sex, but she hadn't remembered it feeling so amazing. "Xander, you feel so good. I-I'm…" Her body locked in ecstasy. She froze, wailing from the ardent release.

"Give it to me, babe. I'm coming too." Xander yowled and

forced his hips up. He twitched inside her as her walls quivered around him.

She lay her head on his shoulder, gasping. He caressed her back until their breaths returned to normal. "You're amazing, Xander."

"So are you."

She lifted her head and pecked all over his face. "My husband." She settled an affectionate kiss on his lips and sat back. "We didn't even make it to the bedroom."

He laughed, tapping her bottom for her to get up. "No, we didn't." He stood and took her by the hands. "We can always go there now." He walked backward toward the master bedroom doors.

"No break?"

He smirked. "Do you need one?"

"Not yet." She followed him into the bedroom, ready to follow him for the rest of her life.

22

BENI'S ROOM

"Xander, wait!" Zaynab shouted with the last bit of air in her burning lungs. They must be collapsing. She stopped in the middle of the park's dirt path and braced on her knees. Fit joggers swerved around her and continued their way. Further up, Xander's bottom bounced in a pair of jogging pants. The sight of his cute butt usually excited her, but she was too busy holding on for dear life.

Xander turned and jogged back toward her. He bent next to her. Sweat glistened on his forehead. His fitted tee-shirt was moist with sweat, but other than that, he looked just fine, unlike her. "You okay?"

"N-no," she panted. "How much longer are we supposed to do this?"

He looked at his fitness watch. "We have another mile."

She stood straight. "Oh he-he-hell no!" She strode in the direction they came. "I love you. The past two months of marriage have been great, but I'm not going another step."

"I told you that you didn't have to come." The amusement in his voice only added to her mortification. "Here, let me carry you."

She paused and slapped his sweaty arms. "What is with you and carrying me?" She couldn't help but giggle at his smiling face. She lifted her chin and strode down the path. "Just because I'm laughing doesn't mean I'm not mad."

"Yes, it does," he said behind her.

She stared ahead, not giving him the satisfaction of caving to his charm. They had settled into married life quite well, only encountering a few newlywed scuffles involving decorating the house. "Oh, don't forget. We have to stop by the furniture store and pick up Beni's new bed."

"Got ya. When do you think he'll spend the night?"

"I don't know. Hopefully soon, inshaallah. Dr. Shah said to keep having him over for visits with Mansur and Faiza, then see if he's willing to come over without them. Once he's comfortable with just us, then we can move to him spending the night. I want to have his bedroom ready."

They reached the truck, dwarfing the electric cars surrounding it. "I understand. Our home is little man's home too. Are they still coming over tonight?" Xander pushed the ignition.

"Yes, for dinner, which is why I can't be worn down from jogging." She smirked. "You exhausted me enough last night."

"Hey, you're the one who bought the cuffs. I was just abiding by your wishes, wife." They pulled up to the store. Xander and a clerk shoved the box containing Beni's new bed in the back of the truck. "We're all set," Xander said, before closing the trunk door. He got back in the cab. "I'll put it together tonight."

"No, you don't have to. I'm sure he isn't going to want to spend the night."

"Just in case."

She smiled at him. She loved him so much. "You're right."

Once they pulled in front of the apartment, anxiety filled Zaynab's chest. She went straight into the bathroom and worked through the attack. "You're going to be alright," she said to herself in the mirror. The wave passed and she went to work getting the apartment and dinner ready for their guests. Scrubbing always helped to take the edge off. When the doorbell rang, she had everything spotless and chicken machboos in a big pot, waiting to be eaten.

"I got it!" Xander called out. He gave Mansur a big hug after opening the door. The friends chattered while the rest of the Saleh family came inside."

"Something smells wonderful," Faiza said.

Zaynab floated from the kitchen, wearing a kaftan and in her bare feet. She hugged Faiza and gave salams. "Is that what I think it is?" she asked, pointing to the giant food container in Faiza's arm.

Faiza set Bushra on the floor and lifted it. "Yup. Baked macaroni and cheese, as requested."

Beni tugged at Zaynab's kaftan. "Mommy Zay, listen. He swayed in place and sang the Arabic alphabet. Her heart skipped. She was no longer a stranger to him.

Zaynab clapped her hands when he finished and picked him up. "Alhamdulillah. You're so smart! Are you hungry?"

He squeezed her neck hard. "Yes."

She carried him into the kitchen. "You can help me get dinner on the table."

Bushra crawled after Mansur and Xander as they walked to the dining room. "Get the baby, Mansur." Faiza put the container on the kitchen counter and rushed back out. "Never mind, I got her." She left Zaynab and Beni in the kitchen.

Zaynab kept her anxiety under control while she and Beni put food in serving dishes. Beni sang the alphabet repeatedly and put flatware and cups on the table. Everyone praised him for his solid work. Zaynab put dinner in the middle of the table and sat. Beni sat between her and Faiza. Zaynab fed him.

After dessert, Zaynab showed Beni his new room full of toys and his brand-new bed. "This is for you, sweetie." He bounced around, playing with her until he yawned and stretched. "Okay, let's go." She brought him back to the living room. Mansur and Faiza sat on the couch. Faiza's head lay on Mansur's shoulder while he talked to Xander, who sat in the side share. Bushra lay sprawled on her father's chest, fast asleep. "I'm sorry. I kept you late playing with Beni."

Faiza sat up and stretched. "No, it's fine." She stifled a yawn with the back of her hand. "But we better get going. They all rose. Faiza reached a hand toward Beni. "Come on, Beni. Say salams to Mommy Zay and Xander."

Beni hugged Zaynab's leg. "I want to stay. I have a room."

Zaynab widened her eyes and met Xander's gaze. He smiled. "I'm glad I put that bed together."

Mansur and Faiza looked at each other. "Are you sure, sweetie?" Faiza crouched in front of Beni.

"Yes." Beni pulled Faiza's hand. "Come see, Mommy." She followed him.

Zaynab faced Mansur. "I'm so sorry. I wasn't trying to get him to stay tonight."

Mansur grinned. "It's not a problem. We talked about it before, and we trust you with him. You're his mother. There might be a problem though once he realizes we're gone."

Xander put an arm around Zaynab. "We can handle it."

He stuffed his feet in a pair of sliders and picked up Bushra's diaper bag. "Then you guys have Beni tonight. Let's go Faiza."

Zaynab stood stunned as she watched Faiza and Mansur get in the car with Bushra and pull out of the parking lot.

"Mommy Zay. I gotta potty." Beni ran to her.

"Okay, sweetie. Let's go." A jog through the park with

Xander was nothing compared to taking care of Beni and getting him bathed and in bed for the night. At first, Beni whined to go home, but she and Xander calmed him. Every muscle ached when she finally got him asleep. Nothing felt better than standing with Xander and seeing Beni laying in the bed like an angel. She closed the door and crept with Xander to their bedroom. "Man." She yawned and stretched. "That was rough."

"It sure was." Xander unzipped his pants and let them fall to the floor.

Zaynab got her robe from the hook on the bedroom door. "I love it, though." She walked to the master bathroom.

"What are you doing?" Xander sauntered to her.

"I'm about to take a shower."

He kissed her lips then her jaw. "Want some company?" He made a trail of pecks to her ear and nibbled it.

"Something tells me that we won't get clean."

He turned on the bathroom light. "Oh, we will eventually." He slung the robe over his arm and pulled her inside.

Alhamdulillah, she had her husband and son.

THANKS FOR READING!

I hope you enjoyed Zaynab and Xander's story. Please leave a review on Amazon and Goodreads, so I can continue to bring readers stories! I hope to get more romances to everyone soon!

CONTACT ME

I would love to hear from you.
Email - laylafied@gmail.com
Website - www.laylawriteslove.com

FOLLOW ME

Facebook
https://www.facebook.com/laylawriteslove/
Instagram
https://www.instagram.com/laylawriteslove/
Twitter
https://twitter.com/laylawriteslove
Amazon
https://amazon.com/author/laylawriteslove

MORE LYNDELL WILLIAMS BOOKS

Brothers in Law Series

Open to Love Series

Ramadan Nights Series

BONUS READ

THE GROOM

The Groom – Excerpt
If you enjoyed *The Ex-Wife*,
check out Mansur and Faiza's story!

1

ALARM CLOCK

Mansur yawned and stretched his legs, pushing free the sheets at the bottom of the bed with his foot. He grumbled at the blaring screech from the nightstand. Its shrill sound was the only thing drowning out the screams coming from down the hall. He cleared his throat. "Zaynab," he got out with a croak. He reached across the mattress, searching for a petite form that should have been curled next to him. Nothing but coolness greeted him. *She must be up all ready to take care of Beni.*

He picked up his phone, reading the clock before tucking his head back under the floral goose down comforter. He had set the alarm early so there was time to get some action before work, but no wife, no action. Why did he even think there would be? Things had been so strained between them for months and always ran hot and cold between them. Last night was arctic, but he had hoped for a little makeup sex after all the stress. *I might as well catch a few more minutes.*

After the baby's yowls got stronger, Mansur grunted and cracked his eyelids and peeked from under the blanket.

"Zaynab?" He called louder; only more wails answered him. Man, that boy had a set of lungs. He threw the comforter to the side, swinging protesting limbs over the edge of the bed. His feet crinkled from the coolness traveling up them and the sense that things were off. Zaynab never allowed the baby to cry for so long. He stood straight, yawning, and stretching before surveying the room. Some of Zaynab's drawers lay open across the master bedroom with clothes hanging from them. He squinted. Zaynab wouldn't even let him leave a sock on the floor. Something was wrong.

Beni's screams demanded his attention. He tucked his phone in his pajama pocket and padded down the hall, squinting at the sunlight flooding from the window at the end. He turned into the small nursery. Beni stood inside his crib. Tears flowed down his chubby light brown cheeks. The redness bursting from the top of his head and down his neck gave him a burgundy tint. "Okay, Little Man" Mansur reached over the oak railing and taking his son into his arms. He pressed at the baby's diaper over his Onesie pajamas with koala bears all over them "Wow, this thing is loaded. No wonder you're so cranky," he said to Beni in as soothing a tone as his baritone voice allowed.

He carried Beni's hefty infant body to the changing table and flipped a diaper from the holder. "I got you." The urge to pee and experience getting squirted by Beni prompted him to work fast. "So—" he smiled down at the giggling face, now a more proper complexion "—do you have any idea where your mother is?" The expression of clueless bliss plastered across the youngest Saleh family member sent the clear message that he did not know. Mansur kept smiling despite the nagging feeling that he needed to find Zaynab. The fight they had the previous night was not a pretty one. He had to apologize and then get to his new job.

Mansur dropped the dirty diaper into the pail and zipped up the pajamas before swinging Beni into the air and spinning on the round rug decorated with cartoon animals. Plump arms and legs flayed out above him. He could not help the hearty chuckles seeing his son always primed from him. His boy was the joy of his life.

He tossed the baby's giggling body over his shoulder and made his way down the stairs and into the kitchen. Unlike their usual mornings, everything lay cold and quiet. The eye-opening aroma of coffee did not waft up his nose, and there was no sound of anything crackling on the stove. Nothing was there for them, and no one. He scratched at the nerves prickling the back of his neck. Zaynab was acting strange. Was she trying to stick it to him for last night? "Zaynab?" He straddled Beni's legs at his side and started searching the rest of the house. Tension torqued his shoulders. He went from room to room in his parent's home. After going through the downstairs and upstairs again, he stopped in the garage, flicking on the light. His cobalt blue Camaro sat on the far end, next to the empty spot where Zaynab's car should have been. "Now where did she go so early?"

He winced at Beni's fist, yanking his hair. His son's round, black eyes glistened with the promise of another tantrum. "She must have gone to the grocery store. She better get back before I have to leave for work. I'll make us something to eat." He turned half-way toward the door leading to the house but stopped, noticing an envelope under the windshield of his car. He secured the baby on his hip and pulled it free, reading the words *I'm Sorry* smeared across the front in Zaynab's handwriting. "Crap." What was inside could not be good.

He stomped into the kitchen and strapped Beni in his highchair, dropping a few animal crackers on the tray to prevent another crying bout. The baby grabbed a bunch and crammed them against his face, just missing his open mouth. Disaster averted.

Mansur leaned against the counter and flipped the envelope back and forth. Zaynab couldn't possibly be pulling the fleeing spouse routine, not now. "I just got my act together. I stopped drinking months ago and am even praying five times a day again. Why in the hell would she bail on us? Drama, that's why. It was her middle name. She always tried to make things harder than they had to be. It was a never-ending roller-coaster with her."

His phone's alarm twittered in his pocket, the second warning that he had to get to his new job. He read the time, pacing back and forth along the counter. "Damn it, Zaynab. Who's going to watch Beni?" He threw a few more crackers on the now empty tray and walked to the window, scrolling through his contacts. Names whizzed by with reasons none of them could take care of Beni.

Om—in the Gulf with Abo for at least four months
Rachel—Big Sis lives three states away with her own brood.
Their working.
Working.
Working.
Oh, hell no!

Mansur ran his fingers through his hair, clenching the strands at the top. The time in the upper right corner of his phone raced by. He would lose the only gig he got in a while. "What am I going to do." He glanced out the window, catching sight of their neighbor Faiza across the street, getting out of her crimson Jeep. She straightened and stretched before turning and strolling up the walkway to her townhouse. He bolted outside. "Faiza!" Beni's crying stopped him on the slate landing. She continued, her full hips swaying in beige turnout pants with red suspenders hanging around them. "Faiza, wait!" he screamed over the roar of a garbage truck cruising down the road and blocking his view of her. Relief washed over him when it passed and he saw her standing at the end of the driveway, frowning in his direction. He held up a finger. "Just a sec." He strode through the house and picked up Beni before dashing back out.

2

BREAST MILK

*H*e padded in his bare feet over the pavement, stopping in front of Faiza's. The knitted eyebrows over her oval black eyes made her look just as cute as ever. He dipped his head and hiked the baby further up his waist. "As-salam alaykum. Thanks for waiting," he panted.

Her expression softened before she turned her head to one side and returned his salams. "Is everything okay?"

"Yeah, I mean, no. Zaynab was gone when I woke up this morning."

She frowned again. "What do you mean, gone?"

"Gone, as in not in the house. Her drawers were all open, and her car was not in the garage."

"Do you think something happened to her?"

"No. She left a letter, but I didn't have time to read it. I need to get to my new job."

She tilted her head, framed in a plain, navy one-piece hijab and squinted at him and Beni. "Your new job, huh? Look, Mansur—"

"If I'm ready and leave in—" he looked at his phone "—twenty minutes, I'll make it. I don't want to be late my first day. Please, Faiza." He gave the saddest puppy dog face he could muster. It had to work or else he wouldn't be.

"Where's your mother?"

"She's overseas with Abo."

"I worked two shifts. I'm exhausted."

"You know that you're the only other person we trust with Beni? Don't you want to make sure he's with someone who loves him?"

Faiza sighed and smiled at Beni. "Do you want to stay with Auntie?" The baby reached his arms out. She rolled up her long-sleeve t-shirt with the words *Mastic Fire Department* brandished in the upper left corner. "Give him to me."

Mansur released the baby and turned. "Thanks. I'll get a diaper bag and his food."

"No. Then you'll still be late. I'll come with you and put the stuff together while you get dressed."

She didn't have to tell him twice. Mansur flew into the house and up the stairs, hitting the bathroom. Months of job searching had him worried about mounting bills and feeling like the family bum. The market for history adjuncts had been slim, leaving him to look anywhere for work. Luckily, a position became available at the local Islamic school.

He hopped out of the shower and wrapped a towel around his waist before pulling a pair of black denim pants from the drawer and a white shirt off the closet hanger. The first day of school required making a good impression. No teacher wants to wear the wrong clothes for kids to use to against them. He laid them and a beige jacket-cut cardigan with black button next to them. Soft tapping at the door caught his attention.

"*Mansur.*" Faiza's voice floated inside.

He opened it. "I'm almost ready."

Her eyes widened and mouth hung agape. "Oh, um, that's

nice." She spun on her socked feet. "I have everything Beni will need."

"What about breast milk? How are you going to feed him?" He trailed her.

"I got some out of the freezer in the garage there's a ton." She walked a little faster. "You didn't know?" She practically flew down the stairs.

He followed. "No. That's good then. Do you need anything else?"

She scratched her forehead and opened the refrigerator. "Yeah, for you to put some clothes on."

He smirked. "What's the problem? You've seen me like this before."

She peeked from behind the fridge. "When we were ten and by the pool. Now—" her gaze moved up his body. "You're a grown man with a whole wife. Clothes."

He laughed and turned. Flustering her was always a good time. After dressing, he descended the stairs again, tugging his shirt cuff to stretch the fabric bunched inside his cardigan. "I think I'll just make it." He raised his head to an empty great room. "Okay. That was fast." He grabbed the car keys and spied the envelop Zaynab left. No. Opening that would only lead to hours of overthinking. He needed to concentrate on making his first day a productive one. The engine purred after the click of a button. Its sound grew louder once he was in the garage. The double garage door ground open. He got in and backed onto the road. The only way to stabilize the emotions raging within him was to put his mind on teaching. "Let's go inspire the future," he said as he drove down the street. Zaynab and her drama would have to wait.

3

JUST ACROSS THE STREET

"Bismillah." Faiza entered her childhood home with a diaper bag swinging behind her back and Beni bouncing on her hip. "First, let's get you some milk." She took the big freezer bag loaded with smaller breastmilk-filled packets. She put one in a jar of hot water and set a bottle on black counter sitting on the white glass kitchen island. A quick inspection of Beni's chubby neck folds revealed sticky bits of crumbs and spit. "Yuck."

She brought him into the bedroom and laid him in the middle of the lavender pinch pleat ruffled comforter. He was such a cute little butterball, the spitting image of his father. She couldn't say no to either of them.

Beni rolled onto his stomach. "Oh, no you don't." She turned him on his back, tickling him with one hand, and unzipping the bag with the other. "You need changing." She crinkled her nose and got busy with the stinky task. The baby would probably fuss after a while. He was close to his mother. Zaynab gone was going to be easy.

She had noticed the envelope on the counter, unopened. As usual, Mansur was avoiding the situation, but it wasn't totally his fault. He had to go to work. It took some struggled, but she changed Beni and wiped the sticky residue from his face, neck and hands. Not bad for a childless, single woman. A yawn forced its way past her lips, interrupting her smile of accomplishment. She squirmed in her grimy turnout pants. Almost two days of running around the city for a bunch of tiny emergencies had drained her. She put her palms on her hips. "So, Auntie really needs a shower." He laughed and rolled again, crawling to the other side of the bed. She pulled his little feet. "You're no help." She sat him on the floor and dropped a bunch of big pillows around him, building a makeshift fort that would provide no security. She turned on the widescreen TV bolted to the gray wall. Finding a show with puppets or cartoon characters was easy enough. Soon, Beni sat in the middle of the pillows, mesmerized at the flashing screen.

She dashed into the kitchen and filled the bottle with the melted breast milk, twisting the cap tight on her way to the bedroom. Beni still focused on the puppets. "Okay, you know our deal." She stacked some pillows and leaned him back on them, ramming the bottle into his mouth. That should give her at least five minutes. Beni ignored the world when he was draining a bottle.

She went into the bathroom and peeled off her clothes while happy rhyming songs filtered through the small crack she left in the door. Warm water was just the thing to ease the aches and pains of the night shift. She closed her eyes, allowing visions of Mansur to form in the darkness. He was so sexy, only in a towel, muscular chest glistening. The perfect amount of hair traveled down his torso.

He wasn't always fine. When they were kids, he was lanky and awkward, but then spent one summer visiting his grandparents in Kuwait and came back confident and strong with a body for days. For so long, it had been impossible to do the whole "guard your gaze" thing, because he would hover around her smiling and licking his lips with his new beard. He had grown, leaving stuck thinking … no—no more fantasies about him. She grabbed the body wash and puff, peaking out at Beni, bottle still in mouth. A bit of remorse budded in her chest. Here she was babysitting a sweet child and having haram thoughts about his father.

The shower had her floating on air until she dried and dressed, then the need for sleep crept through her. She yawned and stretched in her plaid pajama bottoms and drab olive t-shirt. Beni popped the empty bottle out of his mouth and turned on the pillows. "All done? Okay—" she covered yet another yawn and picked him up "—I fed you. Why don't we take a nice morning nap? Then we can have lunch." She stretched her tired legs on top of the bed and tucked a pillow under her head. Beni pulled on her hips, climbing across her over and over. She sighed. "I guess you won't be napping?" His giggle and smile confirmed that there would be no sleep for her. "Daddy better get home on time.

To read more, grab a copy of *The Groom*, a Ramadan Nights Series novella.

ABOUT LYNDELL WILLIAMS

Lyndell Williams has a B.A. in Historical Studies and Literature, M.A. in Liberal Studies, and an AC in Women and Gender Studies. She presently teaches history as an adjunct instructor.

Williams is a cultural critic with a background in literary criticism specializing in romance. She is the managing editor of the NbA Muslims blog on Patheos, a cultural contributor for Radio Islam USA and a writer for Haute Hijab and About Islam.

She received the Francis Award from The International Association for the Study of Popular Romance (IASPR). Her peer-reviewed journal article, *The Stable Muslim Love Triangle – Triangular Desire in African American Muslim Romance Fiction,* was published in the Journal of Popular Romance Studies.

Lyndell has contributed to multiple anthologies interracial short story collections, including - *Saffron: A Collection of Personal Narratives by Muslim Women*, *Shades of AMBW* and *Shades of BWW*

Printed in Great Britain
by Amazon